Penmorrow

- A Sebastian Trilogy Sequel -

By Janey Rosen

Dear Nikki
Love
Janey x

ISBN-13: 978-1522839989   ISBN-10: 1522839984

This book is dedicated to all my incredible readers, my friends, who make me smile on a daily basis. Thank you for your interaction on social media and for reading my stories. It is also dedicated to my incredible street team, Rosen's Roses. Ladies, I love you all so much! Your support is unwavering and greatly appreciated. Special thanks to Katie, Nikki and Jodie, for beta reading and being honest. You helped me to make this a better book. Thanks also to Beth and Jodie; for recounting your childbirth experiences. My toes curled, I can only imagine what you went through! Thanks too to Meghan for giving me the name of my antagonist, it suited him perfectly. Finally, thank you to my husband, family and friends who support me and put up with me.

– Janey x

CHAPTER ONE

"I love you without knowing how, or when, or from where. I love you simply, without problems or pride: I love you in this way because I do not know any other way of loving but this, in which there is no I or you, so intimate that your hand upon my chest is my hand, so intimate that when I fall asleep your eyes close." — Pablo Neruda, 100 Love Sonnets.

CHAPTER TWO

Eighteen months and six days. The day we said 'I do' felt like yesterday. Thirty-seven weeks and four days since Bean was planted in my tummy by the man I loved. Twenty-three hours since that man walked out of my life. Two days until Christmas.

Looking back on the argument, it could be said that I was as much to blame as Sebastian. At the time–as with all these spats between husbands and wives the world over–I was certain that I was in the right; that the great, dominant Lord of Penmorrow was being an absolute shit.

There I stood, overthinking, beneath the spindly arms of the old oak tree, a special landmark on the horizon and in my heart, tracing my fingertips along each of the carved letters of our names. I wasn't so arrogant as to believe that I was always right, or that Sebastian was invariably wrong. Even if he often was. I had tried my best, you see, to be what he'd wanted me to be. What he'd needed me to become. Not naturally submissive it had taken all of Sebastian's stoicism and patience to shape me into a wife who would defer to him in all matters. Now that I really thought about it, I realised that I'd become *her.* Was I any different now to that woman?   Scarlett.   I cleaned the house and lowered my eyes and carried his child and…is that what he had wanted all along–to carve me into another version of her?   Did he regret his past at all?   Did he regret his future?

What hurt me the most, even more than his betrayal, was that he was the one person who knew how I'd suffered.   Death and devastation fracture all of our lives at some point.   Cracks that stay in one's mind and heart until you believe that it is somehow your destiny, your lot in this roller coaster ride called life.

My nails raked a slow, reluctant path down over the crusty bark until they reached S+S+Angel.   How had I not seen it before?   All those times that we had raced the horses up to this point.   Made love on this very spot beneath my feet.   All soiled.   All tainted now.   I hadn't expected the response that he had given.   I didn't want it to be true.   I'd needed to know and dreaded the truth. But there it was, carved by her hand; not his, he'd assured me.   How spiteful I'd been in my attack when I'd learned the truth. Venomous. Hurt.

Turning to face the vista, my home now, the dark foaming sea to my right, a little beyond where the once green cliff spilled over into stormy grey, I took a deep breath and tried hard, I really did, to see this fight for what it was. I loved him, you see. Love, though, was only one piece of the puzzle that was our lives together. With love came forgiveness and reasoning, compromise and understanding. We had so very much to lose, he and I, if this escalated.   Taking one last look back at the old oak tree, at its ever-open arms and steadfast rooting, I steeled myself to do what needed to be done to fix this. I would make the first move, as women invariably had to do, even if I was not in the wrong. After all, I hadn't wanted him to walk out. I'd wanted to talk, to make him understand how he'd hurt me.

With my hands shoved deep in the pockets of my coat, face jutted up to the bracing wind, I waddled back down the incline towards Penmorrow. My wellington boots protected my feet from the cloying dampness of snow but not the biting cold that nibbled my toes. I took it easy, each step a colossal effort, the risk of slipping was real. Creaking of newly fallen snow underfoot, the otherwise soundlessness would be somehow magical if not for my own pants and curses as my right foot skidded away. I righted myself in time and stroked a protective hand over the protruding curve of my stomach.

"Don't worry, Bean," I said, "Mummy's going to be careful. Let's get us both inside the nice warm house and call your daddy. Get the silly, stubborn, infuriating man to come home to us. We're a family. Families work through problems together. I know he loves you very much."

I trudged around to the less grand rear of Penmorrow, somehow always favouring its more humble welcome than the austere seventeenth century grandeur of its frontage. Slipping off a glove with my teeth, I fumbled in my coat pocket for the key, stamping my boots to shake off snow. Once inside, I found the kitchen to be barely a degree or two warmer than outside. The heating was playing up again. This rambling old house was impossible to keep warm, colder still without Sebastian's arms to rub away the chill. I missed him terribly. I wanted him home more than I'd wanted anything before. That's not true. I wanted Joe to be back home with us. *Damn it!* Those people who say that time heals, should be made to spend a day in my shoes and tell me they don't miss him as much today as almost this time two years ago. Christmas was going to be tough.

Above the stove, the old clock traced the afternoon away. At three-forty it was already getting dark, the last vestiges of sun dissolving behind the roof of the stables behind me. Kicking off my boots I closed the door and checked twice that it was securely locked. The place was so remote that I honestly didn't like being there alone. I'd felt safer in my house in Dorset. That reminded me, I needed to call the letting agent and have him extend the current tenancy for another six months. This is how my brain had been throughout my pregnancy: flitting from one thought to another with each beat of my heart. My heart. My heart hurt without my husband. I loved him more than my business, that was a fact. Yes, I was angry but I missed him more than loathed him.

In woollen socks, I padded over the cold flagstones of the kitchen floor, through into the hallway where I picked up the cordless phone handset and speed dialled Sebastian. It was hopeless trying to get a signal on my mobile phone in this weather. I didn't really understand the complexities of 4G but I did know my phone was playing up more often than not.

He answered on the second ring–curt, abrasive. "Elizabeth."

"Hi."

"The baby? You're okay?"

"Bean's fine," I said. "Moving around like mad. I think its foot is trying to rearrange my ribs." My hand rubbed over the sore spot.

Silence.

"Sebastian?"

"I'm here." He was still sulking. *Great.*

I heard a low growl, and then, "why aren't you using the walkie talkie?"

"I forgot to charge it." *Damn thing.*

He sighed. "What good is it if you don't keep it charged."

"You didn't notice my handset wasn't charged. If you'd tried to call me on it, you'd have known."

"Don't be facetious."

My bottom lip jutted out. He was insufferable. "I just want you to come home. You've made your point now. Please."

"I don't know…"

"It's only two days until Christmas. I'm about to have your baby. This is ridiculous and, to be perfectly honest, it's irresponsible and cruel."

"It's nearly three weeks until the baby's due and that's just until your due date," he said, voice clipped and cold.

"Please stop calling Bean 'the baby.' It's not an inanimate object."

"Bean. Very well. In any case, *Bean* is unlikely to make its appearance until the new year. Add a couple of weeks to your due date, don't forget. Why are you alone anyway? I thought Bella was coming home with Ruth and your mother."

"They've been trying to get here but the trains are delayed - snow on the lines or something. I'm on my own, Sebastian, and we don't *know* if I'll go full term or longer. You can't control this, like you do everything else." I sounded whiny and needy, I knew it. Truth was that I was scared in the big house alone. I missed him so much that I could cry.

"This isn't about me wishing to control anything, Elizabeth. This is about a breach of trust. I'm not sure how to feel about things."

"I do trust you."

"No. You don't."

"The letter."

"Yes, Elizabeth. The letter."

The tears came. Oh boy, did they come.

"*Sebastian.* Please try and see things from my viewpoint. You kept a secret from me since the very first day that we met. You *knew* that I would be crushed by that letter and yet you didn't destroy it. Didn't show it to me, tell me about it. And now. Now I can't unread it. Can't pretend that it didn't happen." How I wished that I hadn't found it, that I could live out my days in ignorance.

"I had reason to do so. Had you talked to me rationally, but no. The things you said…the things that *I* said. They can't be unsaid, just the same as you can't unread the letter." A pause. When he next spoke, his voice was scratchy, raw. "Do you think for a minute that it wasn't hell for me? Have you even considered the hell that I suffered?" He sounded as distraught as I.

The truth was that I hadn't considered his feelings at all. If I could take him in my arms, show him that together we'd overcome this. All I could do was hope. Plead.

"I'm sorry for every mean word that I said to you." *You have to believe me.* "If I could take them back I would. Please, Sebastian. Please come home. We'll talk it through, no more judging I promise."

"You'll hear me out?"

"Yes. Yes, I'll hear you out darling. I want to understand."

Another pause.

"I don't know. That you'd believe that I'd intentionally deceived you hurts me, Elizabeth. The fact is that I will never be free of her."

"Scarlett is dead. *Dead.* She can't hurt us any more, Sebastian, unless we allow her to."

Another pause.

"You're right. I can't change my past."

I nodded as I wiped my eyes with my coat sleeve. "I know. I mean, I can't pretend I'm not upset about this. But, we'll talk, really talk." I screwed my eyes shut to block out the image I had of Sebastian never coming home to me. It would be easier to imagine a world without sunrise or birdsong or laughter.

"Very well. I'll come home. What the fuck was I thinking leaving you alone?"

"You will? Tonight?"

"As soon as I can get there, yes."

I sighed softly; relief and a sense of love that was almost too consuming to bear. "You're an arse, that's all."

"An arse?" I could almost feel the quirk of his eyebrow.

"Yes. An arse. My arse."

"Your arse is rather delectable, if I recall. Although it's been far too long since I felt it. Since I took it. Hard...."

With his words, my core clenched and tugged inside me into a tight fist of nerves and need. The pulsing of my bud, moistness, all yearning for Sebastian's touch. He cut the call.

He was coming home. Everything else could wait until after Christmas.

CHAPTER THREE

Sebastian

When the call ended, I found that I could breathe again. The tight band that had constricted my chest for almost two days was loosened, albeit still present.

As I slipped my phone into my pocket, I sank back into the leather armchair and brought a crystal glass to my lips, drinking deeply what little scotch remained there until it was gone. An empty chalice. Bringing the cool glass to my forehead, I rolled it over my brow. I'd had a bloody headache all day. Tension.

Resting the glass on the arm of the chair, I allowed myself a moment, eyes hooded and tired, lids heavy. I could sleep for a week. All around me I could hear gruff chatter, guffaws and banter and deals being done and business cards exchanged. Cigar smoke clung to the collar of my shirt, lapels of my jacket and wound tendrils up my nostrils.

Painted onto the insides of my eyelids I saw Scarlett. She was on her knees at my feet; the very act of submission irritated the shit out of me. We'd talked about it—things needing to change. I didn't feel that way about her any more. The way she'd become had bordered on obsessive, to be perfectly frank. I stupidly believed that she'd taken our chat on board, was trying hard to accept that we wouldn't be together again. Fuck, Libby was barely cold in the ground and my life was hell. I'd had months of it, you see. Illness. Madness.

Now, of course, I knew that my poor darling wife was not insane. She was to be slain by the hand of the evil bitch who right then, at that moment, was on her knees while I brandished her letter, waved it in her face. Pregnant. Scarlett was pregnant. Her inky scrawl on my monogramed paper had delivered the news that her lips daren't speak.

She'd cried and scrabbled at my feet and clawed at my trouser legs as I'd told her I'd see to it that the child was raised by my hand. Penmorrow would be the child's home but it was not a home that Scarlett could continue to share with me any longer. I wouldn't be tricked. She'd been on the pill, she'd said. Even made a big show of leaving packets around on the kitchen counter.

Bullshit!

"Lord De Montfort, Sir, can I get you another single-malt?"

My eyes snapped open. "No. I have to drive. Bring me my overcoat and add the bar tab to my account."

"Of course Sir. Do be careful, the roads are treacherous this evening. Will you be leaving London tonight?"

"Yes. Yes, I will. I'm returning to Cornwall. To Penmorrow."

11

To Elizabeth, though fuck knows how I'll make this right with her.

CHAPTER FOUR

With the last of the Christmas presents neatly wrapped and forming a small pyramid where tomorrow our tree would stand, I had taken myself upstairs for an early night, exhausted but relieved that my husband was on his way home to me. This was another trial that we'd face together. We'd been through worse, with Scarlett's death, with the poisoning of both Sebastian's late wife, Libby, and myself. I'd survived where Libby hadn't. I was strong. I'd be strong for all of us.

We'd almost given up hope of a plumber ever arriving to fix the broken bath in our en-suite, therefore I was languishing instead in the guest bath. Sinking down into almost-too-hot, lavender scented water, I felt tension seep out of my neck and shoulders. My hair clipped up in a scruffy bun, I rested my head against the cool enamel and stared blankly at the wall ahead. Soft candlelight flickered and shadows danced over the pale cream plasterwork. Somewhere far off, a grandfather clock matched my heartbeat before striking nine times. Then all was quiet. Calm. Tick...tock...lulled almost to sleep in this watery womb, Bean unmoving, asleep inside me.

Movement. My eyes flicked left and fixed on the open doorway, beyond to the corridor shrouded in semi-darkness. Nothing there. My heart rate quickened. *Don't be stupid, Beth. Breathe and relax, you're just edgy.* I continued to watch the door until my eyes grew heavy, sleep tugged at the corners of my mind. *Mustn't fall asleep in the bath, five more minutes.* I yawned and adjusted my position, my back aching a little. It was so hard to get comfortable these days. Not long to go.

A creak. My gaze snapped back to the corridor, eyes widening as I tried to focus on the gloom ahead. Shadows. There were shadows where shadows shouldn't be and as I stared at them, one seemed to move ever-so slightly. I was tired, seeing things. Unnerved, I hauled myself with considerable effort from the bath and stepped onto the mat, reaching for a towel which I attempted to wrap around my burgeoning waistline. Another creak. Abandoning the towel, I grabbed my robe and slipped it on. It wasn't the first time that I'd sensed her, Scarlett. At times, her memory haunted my mind. I'd said nothing of it to Sebastian. It was over, wasn't it?

Silence. Tick…tick…the grandfather clock whispered his beat as I trod as lightly as I could to the doorway. I stopped and hesitated. What if someone had gotten into the house? A ridiculous idea. The mind plays tricks on you when tired. With a sharp inhalation, I walked with more confidence than I'd felt, out into the corridor towards our bedroom.

Movement to my right, at the top of the stairs. Holding my breath, I stopped dead and trained my eyes on the single spot where a tall shadow bled from the architrave surrounding the artery leading to the north wing bedrooms. Everything was still, as it should be. My eyes were playing tricks on me. I took two paces forward and reached out a hand, flicking the switch to illuminate the corridor. The entire area was immediately bathed in a gentle golden light. Now that I thought about it, I remembered turning on the lights via the switch at the bottom of the stairs. I would never have left upstairs in semi-darkness before climbing the stairs. Or did I?

My heart clattered in my chest. *Hurry up Sebastian, I don't like this.* A sharp kick to my ribs brought my hand to my bump. "It's okay," I whispered. The ticking of the clock at the foot of the stairs grew louder, my hearing on high alert. Tick...tock...tick...nothing. Silence. A sigh behind me. I spun around and gasped. Nothing there.

"Hello?" My eyes darted along a line of shut doors that stood like sentries guarding the rooms beyond.

Tock...tick...tock. The clock recommenced its steady beat.

There's no such thing as ghosts, there's no such thing as ghosts.

From somewhere beneath me, down in the belly of the house, a peal of laughter, distant, shrill...or was it the old house groaning and settling? My heart pounding in my ears, I tore along the corridor to the master bedroom, threw myself inside and slammed the door, turning the key. There I stood, petrified, shaking, whimpering. Someone was in the house. Someone or something. Rushing to the nightstand, I took the phone handset and pressed Sebastian's number, tapping the wrong number twice before the call connected.

"You've reached the voicemail of Sebastian De Montfort. I'm otherwise engaged. Do leave a message and your telephone number. Repeat the number in case it's unclear the first time and then hang…"

I cut the call. *Why the hell do you need such a long bloody message? Always the control freak.* I dialled Ruth's number, pleading for my best friend and business partner to pick up.

"Hi Beth."

"Ruth. Thank God."

"What's up? Is the baby coming?"

"No. No, it's not that, it's not time yet. Where are you now?"

"We've made it as far as Exeter and just checked into a Travel Lodge. Are you okay?"

Massaging a knot at my temple with my free hand I wondered how to phrase it without sounding as mad as the poison had driven me before Scarlett died. "I'm okay, it's just that I'm alone in the house and I heard noises. I'm scared. I know it's irrational but I felt like someone's here."

"What? Get off the phone and dial 999."

"They'll think I've lost the plot. I'm sure it's just the old house expanding and creaking, pipework or something."

"What kind of noises did you hear? Where are you now?"

"In the bedroom. Creaks, a laugh…"

"A laugh? You heard laughter in the house? Jesus Beth, I've got goose bumps all down my arms now. Where's Sebastian?"

"He's…out."

"Out? Out where? What the hell's he doing going out in this weather, leaving you alone in that haunted house?"

"Ruth! Don't say things like that. Please."

"Like what? That he's left you alone, or that it's a haunted house?"

"Both. Neither. Oh, God. I don't know, I think I'm just tired and edgy. We had a tiff, he left."

"When?"

"Yesterday."

"Yesterday. You've been alone since yesterday and didn't think to tell me until now."

"I thought he'd cool off and come home. He *is* coming home, hopefully tonight if the roads are passable."

"Unlikely, Beth. Shit. Okay, look: if you're genuinely scared that someone's in the house, you need to call the police. We can try and get a cab in a minute but apparently the roads are pretty bad. Especially where you are; the roads are bad enough on a good day, for fuck's sake."

"I know. Don't risk it until the morning, Ruth. It's not good for Mum to be out in the cold either with her chest. Is Bella okay?"

"Your mum and daughter are fine. Your mum's making a cuppa and Bella's on the phone to Theo."

"She's back with him?" I lowered my weight onto the edge of the bed. This was news to me. "Since when? I thought they'd split up."

Her voice lowered. "According to your daughter, this is the real thing. Love."

"Oh, for goodness sake. She's not even twenty yet."

"Try telling her that."

"He's a nice boy, Ruth, but I worry he's too much like his father."

"Marcus The Prick. Yeah, well apparently Theo hardly ever sees his dad now. I think that's why he's not coming to Cornwall for Christmas. It'd be too awkward to be at Penmorrow and not call by the house to see his mum."

"Families." I sighed and shook my head.

"I know. All families are dysfunctional in some way. Shit. Sorry Beth. I know this time of year's hard…"

"Understatement. I'm just trying my best to get through the next few days and then look forward to our little arrival."

Ruth sighed, her tone softened. "I know, love. Look, get some sleep and we'll see you tomorrow. If you're at all worried, call the police, okay?"

"I'll try. Yes, okay."

"Good. I love you, bestie."

"I love you too. Night-night."

Talking with Ruth did make me feel a little better. The bedroom door was locked, Sebastian was on his way home to me and I thought perhaps I'd be able to sleep if I read for a while.

Fighting sleep was futile. Positioned in a semi-prone repose, indigestion my enemy as usual, I finally succumbed.

"Aren't you just the queen now?"

"No. No, Scarlett, leave us be. You can't hurt us any more."

"'Leave us be.' You're pathetic, do you know that? You're so sure that my Lord wants that baby, well let me tell you, lady, he'll go elsewhere when you're fat and the child is screaming all day and all night."

"You're just a bad dream…a nightmare, not real any more."

"Am I? You were stood beneath the oak this afternoon, were you not?"

"Y…yes."

"Yes. I watched you from this very room. I was at the window, if

18

only you'd looked up. I watched as you stood by the oak tree. Did you see my initials scratched beneath yours? Ha! You had no idea. How I laughed at the sight of you. Pathetic. Insignificant. Living a lie… living my life with my Lord."

"I'll wake up and you'll be gone. I'll wake up and you'll be gone."

"Oh, my poor dear girl. Don't you see? This is a nightmare you can't wake from. You see, your letter was the poison that will off you. I'll cry a river, before I see to it that Sebastian joins me in eternity. Two lovers will die. Only one will join me. You. Will. Go. To. Hell. Retribution is coming…"

Thrashing, clawing the duvet, sweating. Two figures now: one bathed in light, one dark. Battling, twisting into a mist that vanished into the shadows. My eyes snapped open.

CHAPTER FIVE

"Darling. There, there, it's me. It's Sebastian."

I fought the demon that had plagued my sleep, hitting, scratching, until two solid arms enveloped me and held me tight. As my eyes opened to the soft rays of dawn, I inhaled his scent and exhaled my fear. "I had a nightmare. All night. The same horrid dream over and over and…"

"I'm home now darling. Fuck. I'm so sorry, forgive me Elizabeth."

"You're really here?" Tears of relief misted my sight as I clung to my husband for dear life. "Never do that to me again, do you hear me? *Never.*" I would think about our problems tomorrow, next week. Not now. *Not now.*

"Never. I'm never leaving you again. We'll work through this together." He tilted his head and pressed his lips to mine, parting them in a tender kiss. When finally we parted, he folded over to gently lay his cheek on my stomach. "Hello little one. This is your father speaking."

I couldn't help but melt, my lips forming a smile at last. "I think Bean is happy to hear your voice."

A swift kick to Sebastian's cheek punctuated my statement. "Whoa! I see we have a little footballer in here," he said, kissing the protrusion. "Or perhaps a ballerina or gymnast. Whatever you are, Daddy loves you very much."

My fingers slipped through Sebastian's thick hair, nails softly raking over his scalp as I looked down at the man I loved. "You're going to be the best daddy this little one could wish for."

With a wolfish grin, Sebastian looked up at me. "I will certainly do my very best. In the meantime, I do believe I should be the best lover that my wife could wish for."

Make-up sex, yes please.

As my teeth bit into my lower lip, I sank down and adjusted my position, my thighs parting as Sebastian ripped the duvet clean off the bed. *Oh my!* Exposed and slick, hyper-stimulated, I forced that man's greedy tongue where I needed it most and, for once, he didn't admonish me for taking the lead. My hands fisted the sheet as the course lapping, biting and sucking had me rocketing towards my release. "Don't stop. Please."

He growled against my clitoris causing just enough vibration to tip me over the edge. With a raspy cry, my entire body convulsed in the most delicious ripples. He held me as I bucked and twisted before finally clinging to my stomach as it cinched almost to the point of pain.

"Fuck. I'm sorry. Are you okay?"

When finally I could speak, I nodded with a rather naughty grin and pulled his mouth to mine. Our kiss was chaste, loving and healing. "I'm fine, silly. It's just that when I come, it makes my tummy tighten a bit."

"Ah." He looked at me and frowned. "Then we need

to be careful. No more orgasms for you from now on."

His playful wink was met with a glare from me. "I don't think so, De Montfort. I'll be the judge of my own body, thank you very much."

"Thank you very much, what?"

"Sir."

He grinned that beautiful, clear-eyed sexy smile that melted my heart. "I love you Lady De Montfort."

"I love you so much more, my Lord."

Our kissing became heated and greedy, our fight temporarily put aside. With great care, Sebastian turned me on the bed and pushed my cheek down into the soft pillow, bottom up, as his erection slid effortlessly into my wetness. As my channel clenched and drew him further inside of me, we were finally rejoined in marriage and in love. A fractured love. Fractures mend in time.

Breakfast was yummy. I ate almost my body weight in smoked salmon and scrambled eggs. For the moment, neither of us spoke about the letter or the argument. Honestly, I welcomed a reprieve from the darkness that had cloaked us both over the past day or two. We would have to face it but I suspected that Sebastian, like me, wanted to focus on getting through the festive holiday.

"I'll get it." Two, three, four loud cracks of iron on wood heralded the noisy arrival of my mother, best friend and daughter. The three most important women in my life were huddled on the front doorstep singing an off-key version of 'Rudolph the Red Nosed Reindeer.'

"You're mad." Clapping my hands together when the scratchy singing stopped, I drew all three into a warm hug as best I could while as big as a house.

"Beth! Oh my God, look at you." Ruth held me at arms' length and laughed. "You're enormous!"

"Gee, thanks," I smirked. "You're meant to say that I'm blooming."

"Blooming enormous." She roared with laughter while Bella pushed past and kissed my cheek.

"Where's Sebi?"

"Go and find him love, he's been dying to see you. He's in the kitchen washing up, believe it or not."

All three looked at me aghast.

"The high-and-mighty lord is washing up. You've broken him in at last," said Ruth.

As I giggled, feeling more relaxed than I could remember, Ruth winked and followed Bella to the kitchen leaving me to hug and kiss Mum again.

"You look lovely, dear," she smiled. "I've knitted so many cardigans for the little one that you wouldn't believe it."

"Mum, you shouldn't have, honestly." I could only imagine the twee designs that she had made and I knew that this baby would be warm but very uncool for its formative years.

"Nonsense. This old house is very droughty and she'll need bonnets and woolly clothes."

"She?"

"Oh, Beth. I've been saying from the start that it's a girl, and look at you. The way you're carrying all up front, it's definitely a little pink one in there." Mum stroked a loving hand over my stomach. "That's why I've knitted everything in rose and buttercup."

"Pink and yellow. Lovely." I rolled my eyes. "Come on, let's go and find His Lordship before Ruth hogs him all to herself."

"Ah, here she is." Sebastian beamed brightly as he scooped my mother into his arms, and held her in a death grip to his chest as she laughed and told him to put her down. "The family is all together at last."

For a little while I simply stood and looked at my family and tried so hard to believe that he was right. The truth was, though, that my family would never all be together again. *Snap out of this, Beth. Joe would want you to be happy today.* And I was. Honestly I was. It's just that there was always a hole that couldn't quite be filled.

"I know that look," Sebastian said as he walked over to me and tipped up my chin, looking down into my eyes with such love. "I *know*." He did know, without saying it, he knew. I saw the pain behind his smile too, just as he saw mine. Two broken souls bonded together with grief and hope and love. Both, in our own way, mourning the loss of a child. It was too dreadful to speak of. Too horrid to think about. Right now we had each other and two very much alive children to think about: Bella and Bean.

"Mum, it's going to be sick. I've got you and Sebi the most epic prezzie." Bella helped herself to a sliver of salmon, dangling it into her mouth like a wriggling worm. "You're going to freak."

"I can hardly wait," I replied with a scrunch of my nose and wide smile. "I can only imagine what you've bought us."

"It's a Bugatti, isn't it?" Sebastian left my side and filled the kettle, placing it onto the range hob.

"Better."

He looked at my daughter with a raised eyebrow. "There is nothing better than a Bugatti. I'm going to be bitterly disappointed with anything that isn't it. Don't ruin my Christmas."

The kitchen erupted into laughter and banter and teasing which Sebastian took good-naturedly. My petulant boy-like-man pretended to mooch off in a huff as everyone else tucked into the rest of the food and I ate another breakfast.

"Come on," I said as Ruth cleared the table. "Let's get our wellies on and go outside. I need to walk off this food."

Ruth squinted and peered out of the window. "I'm not sure Beth. Looks like more snow's on the way. In your condition, you've got to be careful out there."

"Oh phooey," I huffed. "I won't be locked up in this old house like a prisoner. Besides, it'll give Sebastian, Mum and Bella a chance to catch up and I think he could use the company."

"Hmm. Well, it will give you and I some time alone so that you can tell me what's been going on here. Let me go and get my Gerry Webbers on. I draw the line at wellies for fuck's sake."

With Ruth looking like she'd stepped from a fashion shoot in faux fur coat, knee-high leather boots and matching accessories, and me resembling a woolly snow ball, we set off towards the stables. I wanted to check on the horses in this bitterly cold weather, even though Sebastian assured me daily that they were fine. Since we lost our stable boy to a farm near St.Minver, it had fallen upon Sebastian and I to take care of our four-legged friends.

"Hello girl." Aggie snorted and shoved her nose out of the stall to be petted. Sniffing my empty glove she kicked at the stable door, her disappointment at the lack of treats quite evident. "I'm sorry. I'll bring you some treats this afternoon when I come to muck you out."

"That's a new one, isn't it?" Ruth held out a tentative hand and patted the horse's neck.

"Yes," I said, "Sebastian bought her after we lost Zariya. To be honest, he didn't really want another mare but this one kind of claimed us when we went to see her. She followed us around the yard, it was quite sweet. He still misses Zariya so very much."

"I'm sure he does, and I'm sure she's very nice but you cannot muck out horses in your state," gasped Ruth.

"I'm not sick, Ruth. I'm careful and the exercise is good for me."

"What if one kicked you or, I don't know, barged into your tummy?"

I laughed. "Horses don't barge. Besides, I don't ever get too close to Brutus these days. He's less predictable, fiery like his master."

"Speaking of the devil himself, why don't you tell me what's been going on?"

We walked across the yard, over gravel now white and streaked and dirty. The early sun was gone now. Snow clouds gathered, silver and bleak. The gusts and eddies of yesterday had stilled. All about us was hushed, not even the chatter of birds to break the silence. When we reached a low wall separating glistening deer park from snorting horses, we stopped and looked ahead, away from each other.

It was Ruth who spoke first. "Has he been playing away from home?"

"What? No."

"Have you?"

I laughed. A soft circle of mist rose from my lips and vanished. I threw my friend a scowl and shook my head. "It's nothing like that. It's worse, far worse."

CHAPTER SIX

Ruth's eyes widened as she evidently struggled to think of a scenario that could be worse than infidelity between Sebastian and I. "The kid's not his."

Throwing back my head I barked a sardonic laugh. "Oh my God. How could you even think that?"

"Well then, tell me. He wouldn't leave you without reason, Beth."

I thought about my answer, there being no easy way to tell her the enormity of it all or the irony of her joke. Looking over the bobbing heads of deer searching in vain for patches to graze, up to the oak tree, my voice was little more than a whisper. "I found a letter inside a journal in his study."

"You were snooping?"

"No. No, I was interested that's all. In his past, in what he writes when he's locked away in that room of his."

"What did it say?"

"It was a breach of trust. Something that he kept from me."

Ruth sighed. "Tell me. Just spit it out."

"I can't." I wanted to.

"Why?"

"Because Sebastian and I haven't yet talked about it properly together."

"I see. Well, it must have been serious."

"It was."

I could feel the curiosity radiating from Ruth.

"It was about Sebastian and Scarlett. I went down to her room. Sat on her bed and read the letter over and over again. I was angry, Ruth. So angry that we had a huge fight when he got home from Padstow."

Ruth glanced across the deer park then locked her eyes on mine.

"Why her room?"

My eyes met Ruth's. "That's what's strange. Her bedding had been stripped and, along with all her personal effects, burned. I found myself in the cellar–I don't know what drew me there–wandering around the places she'd been. I can't explain it. It was as if Scarlett herself made me go there." I paused and tugged the edges of my coat tighter around me, a chill, bone-cold.

"And I went into her room. I sat there, on her bed. And any calm I'd tried to maintain melted away. It was as though I became someone else. I upended the bed and it smashed her mirror." My eyes searched Ruth's.

"Fuck, Beth."

"I know. It was as if just being there in her old room, she was somehow influencing me."

"Hmm. Tell me what it said, Beth love."

"All I can tell you at the moment is that our fight was full of accusations, of insecurity and spite."

"I still don't understand why he left you. Why didn't

29

you both talk it through?"

"Everything I said pressed his buttons. We were both so angry with each other. I didn't know how to make it right."

"Whatever it is, you have to talk to him, Beth."

"After Christmas. It's hard enough on us all without this. I want to savour what we have."

Ruth's gloved hand rubbed my arm. "No matter what, you're a strong couple. You've faced worse than whatever this is. You'll get through it together."

I wanted to tell her. If I did so, she would be angry, fight with Sebastian too and I wanted this little slice of peace–Christmas.

"I hope so. I want this marriage to work, Ruth. I've dared to believe in fairy tales, that there really are rainbows and that Sebastian is my pot of gold. I won't let anything drive us apart. Not ever."

Right on cue, the tiny one inside of me turned a little roll that forced me to catch my breath. A new and pressing weight settled somewhere low and tender. It brought a smile to my lips and a new resolve to my being. He or she was getting ready to make a grand entrance and deserved a stable home to be born into.

I was a strong woman. There was *nothing* that I would allow to break us. Not Scarlett's memory…or rather, the late Sarah Dorling. Not Sebastian's will or his manipulation.

Linking my arm through Ruth's, we tucked close for warmth and love, and continued our walk through startled deer who scattered with gentle thud of hooves and bobbing tails. As we neared the old oak I steered us away, back towards the house, afraid to go there today; the magic of the tree now tainted.

As we trod a path back home, Ruth talked about our business, Evershaw Dove Recruitment, its performance and our staff. I said little until it became evident that Ruth had something on her mind too. I probed her until finally she acquiesced to my questioning. There had been an approach to buy out the company, she told me. My eyes widened, more so at the figure she mentioned. Wow. It was enough to secure our futures. I would be financially independent of Sebastian, no longer beholden to him. I'd always been independent, had to be, and with another child on the way…I was tempted.

"Who's the interested buyer?" I asked as we reached the house.

"Apparently it's an overseas conglomerate looking to break into the United Kingdom recruitment sector."

"Wow. What's their name, I'll Google them."

"I don't know. I've been approached by a lawyer in London. All very hush-hush. Market sensitivity he said."

"Seems odd. Can you set up a meeting for the first week of January?"

"Tried that. Everything's to be handled through the lawyer, so the meeting would be with him in London."

As I struggled to kick off my wellington boots, finally waving a leg out to Ruth to help, I shrugged. "I don't suppose it will hurt having an initial meeting with the lawyer but we'd need to meet the buyer eventually. I won't sell to just anyone. We're too invested, Ruth. I care about our staff and our company too much to just sell to any Tom, Dick or Harry."

"I agree. My view is that we should turn down the proposal unless the buyer deals with us directly.

Something doesn't feel right about it, Beth."

Struggling not to topple over as Ruth tugged my boot, I said, "Fine. Then we'll go on our gut instincts and say thank you very much, but no. Unless they approach us directly."

"Agreed," Ruth replied. "I'll put a call through in a minute if I can get a signal out here in the sticks."

"Should we let Sebastian know? He is a shareholder, after all."

"Ah, you're back." Sebastian filled the doorway in his ever-imposing manner. His face wore a relaxed smile as his eyes met mine. "I was about to send out a search party."

"Nonsense. We were only gone for half an hour." Now free of my boots, I padded over to him and rose up onto the balls of my feet to plant a kiss on his lips, my hands cupping his stubble-peppered cheeks. "But I'm glad that you missed me."

"I always do, darling. Now, what did you want to tell me?"

I glanced at Ruth. "Oh nothing. I'll tell you later, it's just business."

"All okay at the agency?"

"Yes, fine," said Ruth.

I pursed my lips.

"Elizabeth. Did you remember that the villagers will be arriving soon to deliver our turkey and tree?"

"Yes, Sebastian, I did. Honestly, it's amazing that they give you those completely free."

"So they should," he huffed with a smirk. "It's a tradition going back over four hundred years. Penmorrow has always been the hub of the village, providing a living for land workers and domestics. It's the least they can do to say thank you and show respect."

Ruth coughed behind me. Sebastian glared.

"Sebastian De Montfort. You do realise that you sound like a pompous prick?" My eyes glinted with mischief as I backed away from him. *Oh, you're playing with fire here, Beth.*

"Pompous prick, hmm?"

I nodded and backed myself against the dresser, running my tongue over my bottom lip.

My raging bull dipped his head, snorted and observed me from afar. "Lady Elizabeth De Montfort. Come here, and say that again." Pointing to his feet, his gaze was heated, dark.

Holy crap! "I don't think so."

"You don't...think so?" He looked incredulous. If his jet-dark brows rose any higher they'd disappear into his hairline.

For a second I questioned my own sanity. Waving a red flag at the bull could only end in tears. Mine. The faintest tug of his lips in evident amusement kicked into touch my stubborn side. *Smug bastard.* I shook my head. "No. I don't think so, Sir."

Ruth brushed past us both with a sigh and a chuckle. "Yeah. I think this is my queue to disappear. If I hear screams, I'm calling the police. Just putting that out there."

We were alone. This could go deliciously well, or very badly for me.

"I see." Sebastian stroked his long index finger over his bottom lip and worked his jaw, his gaze not leaving mine. "I'll count to three."

"You can count to a hundred-and-three and I'll still be

stood here." I nodded. Butterflies beat their tiny wings in my stomach, nerves or Bean, I wasn't sure. Adrenaline spiked until my fight-or-flightometre needle struck *danger!*

"One."

"Not moving."

"Two."

"Three," I said on his behalf.

"Oh, Elizabeth, Elizabeth." He rolled his shoulders.

"Yes, Sebastian?" My teeth grazed my bottom lip.

Tipping back his head, Sebastian laughed, the humour not reaching his eyes which remained cloudy, stormy.

"Three."

My palms beat together in a slow clap. *Are you insane?* I couldn't help myself. "The great Lord of Penmorrow can count to three. I'm impressed."

He couldn't look more surprised if the ghosts of a thousand maids had appeared in a naked cha-cha. With his arms by his sides, fingers curling into his palms, my brooding, dangerous man stalked towards me.

My breath caught, heart clattering in my chest, core clenching. My hand rose as he neared me. *Oh my.* "Sebastian. Be reasonable now, I'm pregnant and you're behaving like an animal." I was on the edge of hysteria, fighting back laughter that melded with a desire to be taken roughly by my lover.

Sebastian didn't utter a word but his expression spoke for him. I was in serious trouble. When he closed the space between us, the heat radiating from his torso singed my skin even before he caught my left wrist in his right fist and man-handled me ninety degrees. The rounded edge of the refectory table now dug into my buttocks. *Damn, he was sexy when he was angry.*

Using his knee to part my legs, Sebastian towered over me, unable to smother me with his form - my stomach putting at least a little distance between us. Throwing him my most charming smile, I shifted my weight and scooted back a little until I was sat firmly on the oak table-top. Thighs wide, I smoothed a palm deliberately slowly over my stomach beneath my long jumper, and slipped my fingers inside the waistband of my rather unattractive maternity jeggings. With great care and considerable effort, I lowered myself back until I was supine, needy and slick. "Why don't you punish your naughty girl?" My fingers toyed with my clitoris; languid strokes and circles that had me moaning out as my eyelids half closed. "Please." I couldn't hold this position much longer, Bean already shifting its weight onto my bladder. "Please." More desperate this time.

With the deftness of a seasoned pro, Sebastian strode to the kitchen door and slid across a bolt that he'd fitted himself precisely for the purpose of taking me in the kitchen. He removed my lower garments as I slipped an arm behind my head and watched him through hooded eyes.

Falling to his knees, he buried his face between my thighs, lathing me with his tongue. This was too good to be true. I knew that I was to be punished and only hoped that I could chase out an orgasm before he decided to withhold it from me. I needn't have worried. It was only moments more before I bit down on my lip and shuddered as waves of pleasure built and grew and rippled out from core to limbs. Pulse after pulse. Still he lathed and sucked and fucked me with his tongue. "No more. Please... Sebastian, stop." He didn't stop. I was going to come undone again and I didn't think that I could stand it. My stomach tightened as my nipples pinched painfully under the confines of my bra. *I see your game, De Montfort.* So this was to be my punishment.

With a guttural growl, Sebastian snapped his head away just as my body succumbed to another release that left me gasping and thrashing on the table. My back sore, the need to pee, urgent, it was a relief when he eased me up and brought me into his arms. Holding me until my body settled, I was grateful that this obstreperous man had shown me clemency. I knew he was capable of far worse.

With his lips pressed to my ear, Sebastian whispered, "stand up. Turn around and carefully lean forward over the table my darling. If you thought that I was a lenient fool, you really don't know me at all."

CHAPTER SEVEN

He took me and took me hard until I was boneless. Spent. Remorseful yet sated as never before.

It wasn't until we rejoined our guests in the morning room some time later—when I could breathe and walk again—that I realised how obvious it was that our time spent in the kitchen had not been cookery-related.

"Something wrong?"

Mother tutted and sighed, returning her attention to a crossword with a raised brow.

"You're gross. I want to puke," said Bella.

I glared at my daughter, cheeks heating. Ruth, however, gave us both a sly wink with a shake of her head, fiery curls bobbing as she sniggered and set down her Kindle.

Sebastian was of course oblivious, or didn't care. Knelt before the hearth, he threw on a couple of logs and prodded at them with a poker. I walked over to the window and gazed out at the noon vista. Snow was whipping through and over trees and land in a horizontal mist that settled in deep drifts against wall and hedgerow. My breath fogged the glass. I wiped a circle with my sleeve and held my breath, squinting through as movement caught my eye.

A figure, bent low against the blizzard, traversed the drive in a zig-zag path on a course for Penmorrow's entrance.

"Sebastian. Are you expecting anyone, beside the locals with the tree and turkey?"

"Hmm?"

I glanced over my shoulder. "There's someone coming."

He pushed to his feet and strolled over to me with a wide smile. *Oh my,* his hair was ruffled, just-fucked. I had an urge to tangle my fingers in it. When he reached me he placed a hand on the small of my back and leant over my shoulder to peer through the foggy glass. His scent - sandalwood and sex. Delicious. "No idea who that is. Stay here where it's warm, I'll go and see."

If I craned my neck, I could just about see Sebastian step out from the porch into the ensuing blizzard. The man was slightly built, wiry even and barely dressed for the elements in nothing more than scruffy jeans and beige sweater. He had to be freezing, wet. With a frown I hurried through to the hall and hovered by the front door, wrapping my arms around my bump in an attempt to keep us from the ice wind that whipped the ends of my hair over my face.

After a few minutes I had decided to call out to bring the man inside. At that moment, Sebastian turned and ushered him into the porch where both men stamped the snow from their shoes and brushed flakes onto the stone slabs. I quickly swung the heavy door shut using considerable effort. My stomach was tight, the modest exertion leaving me breathless.

"Darling, this is Damon."

Extending my hand towards the man, I smiled and said, "hello Damon, I'm Beth."

His hand was icy, fragile. Brittle-bone fingers curled around mine in a weak handshake. This man needed a hot nourishing meal inside him. "Pleased to meet you Beth. I'm very sorry to intrude upon you both like this but my car broke down half a mile up the lane and I was beginning to think I'd freeze to death in some ditch."

"Oh goodness," I replied. "Then it's lucky that you found us, we're not easy to spot from the lane. Where were you driving to?"

"Lands End to see my family for Christmas." The man frowned and chewed his lip. "The roads are awful. Doesn't look like I'll make it in time before dark."

Sebastian ran a hand through his hair, damp curls gathering in clumps around his temples. "I'm afraid I don't know a bloody thing about cars other than I like to drive them. I can have the garage come out and take a look."

"Would you?"

"Certainly." Sebastian turned to me. "Elizabeth, why don't you take Damon through to the kitchen and put the kettle on. Let's see if we can thaw the poor chap while I call the garage."

"It's Christmas Eve. Do you think someone will be there to call out?"

"It's worth a shot."

"Come on," I said to Damon. "Tea or coffee?"

"Tea would be lovely if it's not too much trouble."

"No trouble at all."

Together we walked past the foot of the staircase and into the kitchen. "You'll have to excuse the mess."

"Who's this?"

I turned to see Bella leaning against the doorframe surveying Damon with a smirk. Damon had to be at least mid to late twenties, possibly thirty. "Sweetheart, this is Damon. His car's broken down, Sebastian's trying to get hold of the garage to come and mend it." Turning to Damon, "Damon this is my daughter Bella. She's at uni and has a boyfriend." *Yes, okay. That last part was not absolutely necessary but I know that look on my daughter's face.*

Bella locked her eyes on mine in a 'what-the-hell' glare. I smiled and filled the kettle, placing it on the hob, then watched as Damon hesitated and nodded at Bella.

"Hi Bella, sorry to intrude on family time."

"That's okay," she said a little too quickly for my liking.

I frowned. "Bella, why don't you go and ask Nan and Aunt Ruth if they'd like a cuppa?"

She sloped off with a roll of her eyes. My attention returned to the young man, my gaze drifting from his mop of raven-black hair, scattering of black down that peppered the soft chisel of his jaw, down to the slim cut of his form. I could see why he would be attractive to my daughter. While not classically handsome, he had a bad-boy Romany look to him with honeyed hazel irises that seemed to cut through, to look right inside their target.

"This is so kind of you to welcome me into your home, Beth."

"That's okay." Setting out china mugs. "We wouldn't dream of letting you freeze in a ditch, you might scare the deer." I threw him a grin.

The man laughed before settling those eyes on my

stomach. It wasn't a glance. He frowned. My hand instinctively stroked over Bean as the kettle whistled behind me.

Nodding his head towards my girth, he asked, "when's it due?"

"January."

"Boy or girl?"

"We don't know. We wanted it to be a surprise."

"Ah." Still he stared.

I turned my back to him and prepared the pot of tea, for some reason I was uncomfortable alone with him. Irrational pregnancy hormones.

"Big age gap…between Bella and the baby I mean. Accident?"

"I beg your pardon?" My lips pursed.

Damon raised his hands. "I'm sorry. I didn't mean any disrespect, I'm always too outspoken according to my parents." His face softened.

"That's alright. Could you carry the tray through for me please?"

Leading the way to the morning room, I replied, "it wasn't an accident, no. This baby was much longed for." With no intention of sharing more than that, we entered the room and I introduced the stranger to Ruth and mother, noting how Bella's eyes drank him in.

Ruth poured the tea while I sank heavily into an armchair.

"You look done in, Beth love. Why don't you go and lie down for an hour or two? I'll make us all some lunch in a while and give you a shout when it's ready."

"The villagers are coming with the turkey and tree. I don't want to miss it."

"You won't. Sebastian said they're coming at two-thirty. Go on, scram."

I didn't need telling twice, I was exhausted and uncomfortable. "Damon, please excuse me. I'm sure Sebastian will be back down in a minute and hopefully you'll be able to be on your way in no time."

Something crossed over his eyes, something dark. My imagination perhaps as it was as quickly replaced by a warm smile. "Let's hope so. Mum will be gutted if I can't get there for this evening's family party. Thank you. Hope you get some rest."

With a polite nod I wished him a happy Christmas and climbed the stairs. In our bedroom I found Sebastian replacing the telephone handset in its cradle. "Any luck?"

With a sigh he shook his head. "Nope. Not a hope in hell of getting anyone out until after Boxing Day. I asked him if he was a member of a motoring organisation, sadly he's not. Nor am I."

"Shit."

"Language."

I couldn't resist sticking out my tongue as I lowered my enormous self onto the bed with a sigh of contentment.

"Darling," he said as he towered over me with that glint in his eye that was one hundred percent danger. "If you weren't the size of a small house I'd have you over my knee right about now."

"Weirdo."

His grin widened as his brow quirked. "Oh, you have no idea how weird I can be. Don't for a minute think you've seen the bad arse in me yet."

"Ass."

"Ass?" His eyes widened, teeth grazing his lip.

"It's badass not bad arse. You're too upper class to be street-cool."

Sebastian chuckled and leant down to kiss my petulant mouth. A chaste kiss. "You do know that I'm keeping a log of all your infractions my darling?"

Well damn. "You are? Where do you keep it?"

One long finger tapped his temple. "Right up here. And I never forget."

"You're an elephant."

"And you're a mouse. I suggest when the baby's born you run and hide in a hidey-hole because payback will be a bitch."

Oh, good lord! Sinking into the pillows, hand slapped to my mouth to stifle a giggle, I shook my head. "Hidey-hole?"

He gave a sharp affirming nod. "And in the meantime, Lady De Montfort, rest. I'll sort out our visitor and make sure I somehow get him back on the road."

"How?"

"I've no idea yet. I'll make some calls, see if I can either find a rental or, if necessary, have someone drive him. We can't have anyone missing Christmas with their family."

I'm melting. "You have a heart of gold, my lovely husband."

"Don't tell anyone. I have a mean reputation to live down to."

I knew differently. Alone now, I pulled several pillows from a stack and shoved them about me until semi-comfortable. Finally, I succumbed to sleep.

No. Don't touch her. Bella! Bella run. Run fast. I can't...

ground is sticky…glue…blood…oh my God. The carpet is soaked, I'll never get it out. Red.

"Beth. This way."

"Ruth?"

"Bethie…this way."

"Who is it?"

"Me. Libby."

"No…."

"Beth, wake up sleepy-head. Lunch is ready."

CHAPTER EIGHT

Sebastian

I wasn't an animal though some might say the opposite, my wife included. It was about claiming her again. I knew Elizabeth better than she knew herself and her need to be taken was linked to vulnerability rather than desire. Did this irk me? No. I liked to think that I was in tune with the complexities of the fairer sex and I'd be a liar if I didn't admit that one hoped that one would be forgiven his transgression a damn sight easier if he satisfied his woman. And satisfy her I did. And then some, as they say.

She'd not mentioned the letter or the fight or the pregnancy and for that I was more than grateful. Surprised, yes, but relieved more so. It was fortunate for me that Christmas was upon us - the time of goodwill to all men evidently rang true in our household. Christmas had never held any grandiose appeal to me. I'd passed too many of the retched things in the morose company of my mother after Father died, to extricate any semblance of pleasure from the proceedings. On this occasion, however, I was glad of it. Of the festive spirit and parking aside of spats and disputes.

It didn't bother me that a stranger had entered my home because, in doing so, he had added a further distraction to events. He seemed a decent fellow if a little common. I didn't doubt that he had the potential to be lewd and licentious; I'd keep an eye on him, particularly around Bella. One wrong footing and I'd have his hide out of the door. My step-daughter would remain a spinster if I had my way. It was bad enough that Marcus's boy was still sniffing around her like a starving dog chasing a lamb shank. I knew his father too damn well and didn't doubt that his rotten genes had harvested a rotten crop in his offspring.

The aromas emanating from the kitchen were, quite frankly, making my stomach growl. The thought of food burned almost as fierce in my mind as the notion of correcting Elizabeth in due course, after the baby, for all the attitude that she'd given me over the past few weeks. I was a patient man. I'd proven this fact by my self-restraint when, quite frequently, I'd forced back a strong urge to take her over my knee. I'd suffered greatly, truth be told, having to rein in my urges and needs during her pregnancy but I'd have my day. Every dog has his day and mine would be one hell of a day. She wouldn't sit down for a month of Sundays once she was fit again.

In the kitchen I was on the receiving end of barbed looks and prickled glares from Ruth. I had no idea what the fuck went on in that woman's head and I was under no illusion that she'd ever thought me a suitable match for her best friend. We'd garnered a kind of tolerance of one another since Elizabeth's ordeal of eighteen months ago. She was more uptight than a monk sat on a stake. She needed to get laid. I made a mental note to suggest to Elizabeth that we might take Ruth to my London club one evening. I had just the chap in mind for her. The thought of Ruth being hog tied by Oscar Le Souza brought a wry smirk to my lips.

"What's put that shit-eating grin on your face De Montfort?"

"Oh, nothing Ruth. Nothing at all."

CHAPTER NINE

"You look like shit."

Breaking a bread roll into little chunks, I dropped them into a bowl of soup and scowled across the table at Bella. "Thank you. One day, when you've got an alien in your tummy who's shoved your lungs under your shoulder blades and your stomach into your spine, I'll be sure to tell you that you look like shit too. And don't roll your eyes."

"My apologies, Damon," said Sebastian. "The women in my life are somewhat feisty but I assure you that their bark is worse than their bite."

Damon chuckled.

"Did you call your parents, dear?" Mother smiled at him.

"I tried. No signal," he shrugged.

Sebastian set down his spoon and blotted his mouth with a napkin. "I've exhausted every avenue, I'm afraid. Aside from driving you to Land's End myself, it seems as though you're stranded here, my friend."

"Sebastian, you can't drive." My brow furrowed. "Look at it out there."

All eyes fixed upon the window behind us; white edged the small panes, flurries of flakes, grey and gloomy beyond.

"The roads will be treacherous." *It's not safe. Please, don't drive. I can't face another loss, another accident.*

As always, Sebastian intuitively read the fear behind my words. "Stop panicking darling. There's no way the roads will be passable beyond Trivessey. I'm afraid you'll have to bed down here tonight, Damon. See how things are in the morning; perhaps one of your family could drive up tomorrow or I could take you if it's brighter."

"You're too kind," said the man. "I can't possibly impose upon you all. I could walk to the village and try and find a guesthouse."

"On Christmas Eve? In this weather? I won't hear of it. No. It's decided. You'll join us as our guest."

"Sick," said Bella.

"How lovely, the more the merrier," said mother. "Can you play Charades?"

Ruth caught my eye and mouthed, "okay?"

I shrugged. It would have to be.

"What'll we do about the turkey and tree?" asked Ruth.

Sebastian smiled. "There's no blizzard that's kept the village from bringing Penmorrow's tree or the Lord's turkey, not in over four hundred years. It would take more than snow to keep the villagers from their tradition and superstition.

Having scraped the last of his soup from the sides of his dish with bread, Damon patted his stomach and looked at each of us. "What's this? They bring you a tree and turkey?"

With a roll of my eyes I nodded. "Every year. I swear

we're back in the middle ages, honestly. They think their crops won't grow or world famine and disease will strike them all dead if they don't give freebies to His Lordship, here."

Sebastian roared with laughter and reached out to squeeze my hand. "Elizabeth. If I don't get my free tree and turkey, I may very well bring about the end of their world."

"You're insufferable."

He grinned like a Cheshire cat. "I am. And you wouldn't change me."

"I might." *I wouldn't.*

With a loud scrape, Sebastian shoved back in his chair and stood, clapping his hands together. "Now. Are the mince pies and hot chocolate ready?"

"It's only one-thirty," I said.

"Everything's ready. I just need to put the mince pies in the oven for a few minutes." Ruth collected our plates and dishes, carrying them to the sink. "Bella, you're on washing up duty. Chop-chop."

"I'll just go and put some lipstick on," said my mother.

Damon and Bella helped Ruth. If I wasn't mistaken, that young man's knuckles deliberately brushed against Bella's arm. *Hmm.*

"How's Theo?" I asked, folding my arms over my expanded bust.

Bella cut me a glare. "He's the same as last time you asked me. Why?"

"No reason, love. Just wondered." I chewed my lip, then: "I hope he likes the Ralph Lauren aftershave you bought him."

My eyes were trained on Damon's back as he dried the

plates that Ruth washed. He tensed, his spine ram-rod straight.

Bella pursed her lips. She'd had her right nostril pierced in the summer, a small diamond glinted under the artificial light. It still looked common, I had't got used to it, doubt I ever would. "He'll love it 'cos I gave it him."

"*To* him," I corrected.

"Whatever. Sheesh, you're so moody since you got knocked up."

Let it go, Beth. "I was just saying, that's all. Damon, do you have any siblings?"

There was a pause. "No."

"Ah. Then it's all the more important that we get you home to your mum and dad. They'll miss you."

Damon turned ninety degrees and, chin to chest, looked at me from beneath a heavy brow, fringe tickling the tips of his lashes. "They're used to me being away." He stopped working the towel around a dish, eyes still locked on mine.

"I…I see," I said. My fingers rose to toy with the choker at my throat, fingertips stroking over the soft velvet. "Well, I'm sure they'll be worried. You haven't arrived, and the weather is awful. Please try again to call them."

Curving his mouth into a smile that didn't meet his eyes, he said, "I'll do that. You're very thoughtful Beth. Sebastian's a lucky man."

What does that mean? "I'm sorry?"

"To have a wife who is as caring as you. That's all I meant."

"Yeah, he is," Ruth quipped. "He scored a ten when he met our Bethie."

"I'm the lucky one." My voice was little more than a

whisper.

"Yes," said Damon. "Yes, you are. In fact, you're both very lucky. To have each other, I mean. And this perfect family."

My frown deepened. "Yes, I think you're right. I have the best family in the world."

His expression softened. "Family is everything. There's nothing we wouldn't do for our family, is there?"

"Nothing at all."

Damon turned his back to me. A shiver ran up my spine to fizz at my nape. I wanted him gone.

"Hark the herald angels sing, glory to the newborn King…."

Cocooned in a shawl, tucked up close to Sebastian, his arm thrown around my shoulders, we crowded in the porch and beamed as the villagers gathered in front of Penmorrow. Children huddled into parents, clad in scarves, hats and colourful coats now whitened by the softly falling snow. Behind them, hundreds of tiny lights twinkled in bush and tree; a spectacular backdrop with white sheets of deer park beyond. The wind had dissipated, all was hushed, all was still. Voices lifted on puffs of breath, as the most harmonious carols were sung.

I tipped up my chin and smiled at the man I loved with my whole heart. He pressed a kiss to my lips and whispered, "merry Christmas my darling. I love you."

"I love you too, so very much." A happy tear leaked from my eye. Bella linked her arm through mine. Sandwiched between the two most precious people in my life - my daughter and my husband. A gentle breeze blew against my cheek. The hairs on my nape rose. I looked down as something that I couldn't see stroked over my stomach. A feather-light touch. And, as I looked upon the children singing–rosy, cold cheeks, hopeful faces, lives yet to live–I knew. My Joe was with us.

Merry Christmas my sweet boy, I thought. *Mummy misses you so much it hurts. But, you're with us, aren't you? I feel you, Joey. My family is all here with me....*

"Happy?"

I turned to Ruth and nodded with a sob.

"Oh, Beth. I know love. I know." Her gloved hand rubbed my cheek.

I kissed her woolly thumb. "Thank you for always being here for me."

"Happy times are coming, Bethie. Nothing but love and laughter from now on for you. For all of us."

Sniffing back the tears, I smiled and nodded. "I feel it too."

"Ah. Here they come." Pulling his arm free, Sebastian rubbed his leather clad hands and smiled a boyish grin down at me, at Bella and Ruth and my mother and Damon. "This. This is tradition."

With the choir chirping about holly and ivy, so a small procession passed through their midst. Trivessey's town major stepped forward first, resplendent in chains of office and bushy beard, his cheeks as ruddy as his bulbous nose. In his arms was the most enormous turkey I'd ever seen, larger than last year's and I'd have thought that impossible. Behind me, Mother swore at the sight of it. We all burst into fits of laughter much to the chagrin of the mayor.

Following behind the turkey were the boy scouts, like little wooden soldiers they marched forward in two neat lines. Between the lines, supported on sloping shoulders, was our Christmas tree.

"Sick! It's huge," Bella squealed.

"How on earth are we going to decorate that?" I clapped a hand over my mouth in near hysterics when the front scout lost his footing, did the splits, the tree crashing onto snow with the scouts forming a tangle of limbs on top of it. "That beats a fairy on top." *Oh, goodness. I needed this laugh and the scout was embarrassed, not hurt.*

Sebastian being Sebastian, immediately barked orders and soon had the little scouts standing to attention and the tree righted. And so began a military operation to get the tree into the morning room and erected on sentry duty in its stand beside the fireplace. Sadly none of the De Montfort gaudy antiques were wounded in the battle.

With the turkey in the pantry and mince pies distributed, Sebastian and I began to dutifully circulate amongst the villagers who gathered in our home. Warm punch was served in paper cups, Sebastian refusing to 'risk the crystal on the locals.' Honestly, all I could do was roll my eyes.

"And this must be Bella's young man?" said the baker's wife (I forget her name).

"No," I replied. "This is Damon. His car broke down en route to Land's End. I'm afraid he's stuck with us until tomorrow."

Damon smirked. Okay, he smiled, but it was nearly a smirk. "Yes, Lord and Lady De Montfort have been very generous letting me crash at their pad for the night."

"Quite a pad it is too," said Mrs. Baker, picking up a vase and peering at the base. "We nearly didn't make it up here either, even on foot. Blessed roads are a nightmare, ruined my best boots."

"I'm so sorry, they're lovely boots." Moon boots the size of bouncy castles. I relieved her of the vase which was probably more valuable than the bakery itself.

Mrs. Baker squinted at Damon. "You look familiar. Are you related to Thomas Crart of Land's End? He had that very same dark gypsy look about him. Funny business that was. Not sure they ever found him."

Damon scoffed. "No, I assure you I'm no relation to him."

Bean wriggled and pushed at my ribs. *Ouch.*

"What's your family name, then?"

Damon drained his punch cup and glanced at his wristwatch. "I've just remembered I haven't tried to call my parents again. Thank you for reminding me." Crushing the cup in his fist, he hurried from the room.

"Odd sort."

"Isn't he."

CHAPTER TEN

I knew that it was wrong to listen at the door. That Damon had shut himself away in Sebastian's study more than riled me and a hormonal pregnant woman was not one to try and cross. Covering my left ear to shut out the noise of the crowd, I pressed my right ear to the ancient oak door and pursed my lips. I was keeping watch too; this would not look good if someone caught me sneaking around my own home. The Lady of the manor was eavesdropping on her house guest.

Silence.

My brow furrowed. If he couldn't get through to his parents, what was he still doing in there? I thought about all the confidential estate papers littered over Sebastian's desk.

"Whatever are you doing?"

My eyes widened. *Caught!* "Sebastian. You made me jump."

His arms snaked around my waist as he smothered my back with his firm abs and pecs.

Shit!

His mouth close to my ear, breath warm on my neck. "Hmm. Who are you spying on, oh devious wench?" His teeth grazed my earlobe.

Straightening up, I turned to face him, cheeks burning. *I look guilty as sin.* "Spying?" I laughed. "I wasn't spying on anyone, my love. I had a cramp and was just resting until it passed."

Sebastian cupped his palms around the sides of my stomach and quirked a dark brow. Amusement was plainly evident in his twinkling eyes.

Damn you. I can't get a thing past you.

"Is that so? Then I'm very sorry to hear that. You're okay now?"

I nodded quickly and chewed on my lip.

Sebastian scrubbed a hand over his jaw and looked at the closed door to his study. Without another word, he stepped around me and opened the door. I followed him inside.

"Sebastian...no."

"Damon. Did you find what you were looking for?"

The drawer to Sebastian's desk was open wide, Damon stretched languidly back in my husband's chair. The air was thick with tension.

"What the...." Shoving my hands on my hips I scowled at the impudent young man.

"I'm so sorry, Sebastian," said Damon. He looked neither contrite nor alarmed at being caught red handed, doing whatever he'd been doing. Up to no good. "I was looking for a sheet of paper to write you both a thank you note."

"Were you indeed?" Sebastian's voice was clipped, cool.

Oh, this was not going to go well.

"Yes. I can't reach Mum or Dad so I decided to slip away rather than disturb you and try to hitch my way to them."

"I see. In this weather. It will be dark soon too. Do you think that's wise?"

"Sebastian, let him go," I said, slipping my arm through his.

Sebastian held up a hand to shut me up.

"Let Damon speak, Elizabeth."

Rocking forward on the chair, Damon pushed to his feet and slid the drawer closed. I looked up at Sebastian's profile and saw him work his jaw.

"Not wise, no," said Damon. He slid the chair home and walked around the desk. "But I really don't want to outstay my welcome, or to worry my parents. They've not been well."

"I'm dreadfully sorry to hear that. Of course if you wish to go, then go. I'll see to it that you're provided with some food for your journey and I can lend you an overcoat. You can return it on your way back after Christmas."

"My car…I'll need to have it towed."

"Indeed you will."

Both men held the other's stare. It was like a stand-off, a testosterone fuelled duel of unspoken words. In the end, I broke the ensuing silence. "I'll go and make a flask of tea and some sandwiches."

"What's going on?" Bella strolled into the room and looked at each of us in turn with a frown. "You're leaving?"

Finally turning his attention from my husband, Damon

smiled at Bella. "Yeah. I'm going to hitch. If I can find anyone out on the roads in this."

"But you can't." Bella glared up at Sebastian and twirled a dread-like curl around her finger. She knew exactly how to play her step-father. "Sebi, he'll freeze his bollocks off. You can't let him go."

"Language Bella." Sebastian cut her a stern glare. "It's our guest's prerogative to do as he chooses. Penmorrow is not a prison."

"Come and help me in the kitchen please Bella. Sebastian, our guests are probably ready to leave."

"Are you for *real?*" With fists clenched at her side, my daughter looked for all the world as though she were five years old again, mid tantrum. "It's Christmas? You're gonna kick this dude out in the snow because why?"

"I'll go and see to our guests," he said.

"Sebastian?"

"Yes?" His expression was unreadable, brooding as our eyes met.

"Can you make my excuses? Say I'm tired or something."

With a nod of his head, my husband returned to the role of charming host. I turned on my heel and narrowed my eyes at Damon. "Bella, go and start making sandwiches please. There's a ham in the fridge."

Alone now, I bravely took a step closer to the man that I didn't trust. "Who are you?"

"Damon." His lip curled in a half-smile.

"And what do you want with us?"

"Want? Nothing. I really do appreciate your hospitality and I'm sorry to have barged in on your family Christmas."

"Bullshit! Cut the crap. Strangers don't just happen upon Penmorrow and certainly not in the middle of a snow storm on Christmas Eve."

"My car…."

"Your car. Where exactly is your car? I mean…tell me what road and how you managed to stumble upon this house."

"Beth. I get why you're suspicious and I'm sorry." Damon raked a hand through shaggy black hair and smiled at me. "But I assure you I'm not here to rob you or anything."

His eyes were liquid honey. Innocent.

Was I being unreasonable? "What were you really doing in here?"

"I told you. I wanted to write you both a note. I came in here for some peace and quiet to call home and, when I couldn't get a signal, decided to head off. I was looking for some paper. You have a very suspicious mind, Beth."

"Mrs. De Montfort."

"*Lady* De Montfort, isn't it?"

"Don't get smart with me. Be on your way now."

Damon took a wide step towards me. I took two paces back. His eyes misted with a faraway look.

I brought a hand to my throat. "I'll go and see if your sandwiches and tea are ready and I'll ask Sebastian to see you out. I'm…I'm tired. I need to go and lie down." That was a lie, of course. I didn't know what it was about him, other than his intrusion and, well, the unnerving way that he looked at me. I wanted him out of our home.

Who are you? What do you really want here?

My daughter followed me to the kitchen. "Mum, I think you and Sebi are bang out of order."

I glared at Bella and snatched the knife from her hand, quickly cutting the sandwiches she'd made. "I don't care what you think, Bella. I'm not comfortable having a strange man in our home, especially on Christmas Eve."

"What, you think he's an axe murderer?"

"He very well could be." The food was placed into an old ice-cream tub.

Bella slammed a flask of tea down onto the counter before leaning against it, arms crossed. "Sheesh. Ever since the nutty maid, you've been a bag of nerves. We've had our drama, Mum. The poor guy's never gonna find a ride in that."

I followed her line of sight to the snowy vista through the kitchen window and frowned. "I don't care. And, unless you've forgotten, that 'nutty maid' tried to kill me and was responsible for your brother and father's deaths."

"Yeah, like I'd ever forget," she hissed, storming from the room.

Merry Christmas, Beth. Oh my God.

Bean kicked. "Not now," I scolded.

With the last of the guests filing away from Penmorrow, I watched from the bedroom window, forehead pressed to the cold glass. I waited. Waited. Why hadn't he gone yet?

Movement below...Sebastian shaking his hand. Damon dressed in Sebastian's old ski jacket, one of his woollen scarves twisted around the man's neck. Tucked under his arm, Damon carried the parcel of food, in his other, a torch. Another gift from my husband, I thought.

A sharp gust of wind caught a snow drift and whipped it into a frenzy. The man bowed his head, tugged up the jacket collar and turned from the house. I watched him walk away. With each step that he took, so I could breathe a little easier and I couldn't explain why that was.

Behind me a door slammed shut. I glanced over my shoulder. Not our door, another door. A draught perhaps. My eyes snapped back to the window. The eddying snow was still. The driveway empty. The man was gone.

CHAPTER ELEVEN

Sebastian

It has often been said that I am a good judge of character. In Damon's case I knew that he had the potential to be trouble from the outset. What the fuck he was doing in my study, beat me. Yes, he gave some cock-and-bull story about writing us a note of farewell but I also read the damn guilt in the man's eyes the moment I set foot in my study. I didn't like the man. I was more than willing to part with my ski jacket and torch if it meant that we'd seen the back of him. Did I think that he was a lunatic? No. Did I suspect that he'd steal my family silver? Undoubtedly. I'd seen his type time and time again over the years. Tenant farmers tended to breed one of two kinds of human being: the next generation of tenant farmer, or the ne'er-do-wells who thought nothing of sponging off tax payers and robbing blind anyone who showed weakness. Damon was the latter type. Part of me—the invariably dubious corner of my mind—doubted that there even existed a broken-down car at all. Weight had shifted from my shoulders as I'd watched the man traverse the driveway.

Damon, though, was the least of my worries. My wife was pale and her thoughts troubled, I could see it in the small crease that always played over her brow when something colossal was on her mind. The revelation. The letter.

I spent a short while in my study alone after the man's departure and the house had settled back into familiar calmness. I wasn't one for noisy gatherings, never had been. Not like my parents, different in so many ways, alike in others.

How the fuck had she found it, the letter from Scarlett? Where had it been all these years? This desk on which my fingers drummed, the armoire in our room, the davenport in the great hall, in a dusty corner or beneath a pile of estate papers, I had no idea. It was all about damage limitation now, nothing else to be done about it. Bloody mess. Why had I kept it? What was I thinking? *You fool, De Montfort. You fool.*

Across my desk, in a grate set beneath a vast stone hearth, nestled between twin mullion windows against which snow crystals wound their way down glass, flames danced a slow waltz and I could again see her in my mind's eye. At my feet. She came as a package, her and the child. Take the child, take me. The child was a part of her, of her love for me. How could I even contemplate a life with the child but without her? Had I no heart? I laughed out loud, alone with my thoughts. How naive the girl had been to think that I would marry her, replace my darling Libby with a plaything. She'd been more than that though, hadn't she? I'd taken Scarlett to my bed, to my heart and I was to pay the keenest price for that weakness. And so I'd relented and acquiesced and made promises to her that were to never be borne out.

When the child had died inside her the very day that she'd reached the end of her first trimester, the point at which the world and medics deemed a child viable, I'd known then that our relationship was as broken as her heart. I am who I am. I was who I was: callous perhaps; closed and cold by the life I'd led, certainly. On reflection, if losing a baby hadn't been enough of a blow that day, she'd also lost me. I was therefore the catalyst that brought about the subsequent events, the fuel that fed her burning fury that was later to almost destroy Elizabeth. That killed her son, her husband.

I dropped my head in my hands and asked God for forgiveness of my sins, atonement; cleansing of my tainted soul. I asked that he make me a better father to this new child, that he keep it safe from harm, from the curse of Penmorrow.

CHAPTER TWELVE

Even rocked up onto tippy-toes I couldn't reach high enough to place the special bauble. "It's no good, I'll have to let you do it."

"Stubborn woman," Sebastian huffed with a smirk. "When will you learn to listen to me?"

"When you start to tell me things that I don't already know."

"And another strike owed."

Oh, bugger!

I took his proffered hand and stepped down from the small step. Tracing my fingertip over the silver glittery J, I placed it in Sebastian's palm and smiled. "I bought this in London. Joe was only about eighteen months old. We'd taken him and Bella up to see the lights in Regent Street. It was one of the few really lovely family days we all shared. Even Alan said after, what a happy time we'd had."

"I'm sure it was one of many, my darling. Let's put it right at the top, yes?"

"Oh, would you? That would be lovely, thank you."

My enormous giant of a man struggled to reach the very top, in the end hopping up onto the stool. "There we are. Pride of place," he said.

Side by side, we looked up at the tree and marvelled at its splendour. It really was the most spectacular Christmas tree I'd ever seen. Each of the baubles, some old, some new, sparkled and glittered and spun in the soft glow of the adjacent fire. Of course, aristocratic types frowned upon tacky tinsel and fairy lights, of which there were plenty on our tree, each branch laden low.

"Isn't it breathtaking?" I beamed.

"It's certainly…tasteless."

"Rubbish! It's the best tree in the whole world."

"It would look better suited to a whore's boudoir."

"Good heavens," said my mother.

"Oh my gawd!" exclaimed Bella.

Ruth shook her head, tossing a tumble of fiery curls almost the colour of the spitting, crackling flames. I swear that her hair was more orange every time I saw her.

"I love you." I did. More than loved him, if that was possible. Love comprised just four letters. How could the enormity and power of my feelings for him be spelled out in just four letters? He was a dozen letters at least—an entire Welsh town. Cheesy, but true. Far from perfect, but perfect for me. Infuriating and controlling and he'd hurt me, but somehow those faults were tempered by love.

In the hallway, the grandfather clock chimed five. "Can you put the rest of the presents under the tree now Mum?" asked Bella.

I chuckled softly. "I'll do it later. I mean, I'll help Santa later, when you're asleep."

"The only fat man that's allowed in my room is Sebi,"

she said, "and not when I'm asleep. That would just be wrong."

"I am not fat." Sebastian flexed an arm and I have to admit that the sight of his bulging bicep beneath his black sweater did all kinds of things to my insides. "And trust me, I never venture in your room. I value my life too greatly."

The clock chimed once more. "Tell me it's not six o'clock already?" I checked my watch. Five past five.

"Bloody thing needs a good overhaul." Sebastian walked past me to check the clock.

"Yes, it was playing up last night. Kept stopping and starting," I called to him.

"I'll call the man out in the new year."

A sharp draught blew through the door of the morning room. Mother tugged her cardigan tightly around her and called to Sebastian who was tinkering with the clock in the hall. "Sebastian, dear, is there a window open? It's rather chilly even with the fire.

The fire in the grate roared as the cold blast fanned and fuelled the flames until they curled and licked their way up into the chimney flue.

"I'm just checking," he called back.

"So," I said, "the turkey is pretty much ready to go. I'll get up early and make the stuffing, if one of you can peel the spuds and help with the veggies."

Ruth looked up from her Kindle. "Don't expect to see me before nine. I'm not a morning person, Bethie."

"Ha! I know this, bestie, but it's our house, our rules. Besides, I'd like to have everything ready by nine so that we can get to church for the ten o'clock service."

"You're shitting me, right? Church? I'll burn, Beth.

You can all go, I'll stay here and open the fizz."

Mother put down her crossword and scowled at Ruth over the rims of her specs. "Ruth Evershaw. It won't do you any harm at all to go to church with us. Quite honestly, you could do with one or two prayers yourself."

"What?" My dearest friend huffed and puffed up her ample chest with a smirk. "I'm an angel."

Mother, Bella and I chuckled together as Ruth pressed her palms together and looked heavenward.

"Oh, Ruth," I said, "the nearest you'll ever get to God is all the holy spirits you drink.

"Speaking of spirits, weren't we supposed to go to Midnight Mass in the village?"

"No Mum, the weather's too awful to drive and there's no way we're walking."

"That's a shame," said Mother, "I was looking forward to it. Last year we all got a glass of sherry, remember?"

I shook my head with a smile. "And you say Ruth drinks too much. Mum you're seriously becoming a lush."

Bella squawked. "My nan's a lush! Wait till I tell Chloe, that's hilarious."

"You'll tell your best friend no such thing."

"What about the little chapel in Penmorrow's grounds?" asked Mother. "Couldn't we all walk down there, light a few candles and sing some carols?"

"What an excellent idea." Sebastian's voice boomed behind me.

"Sebastian." With a loving smile, I walked to him and put my arms around his waist, nestling my cheek to his chest. "Did you find what was causing the draught?"

"I did. The kitchen door was ajar. The latch seems to be on its last legs. This old house is falling apart."

With a frown I pulled back and looked at him. "That's odd. Why would it have opened?"

Dropping a kiss on my forehead, Sebastian said, "I went to feed to the horses earlier. I can't have shut the door properly on my return."

"It's locked now though?"

"Yes my darling. It's locked. Stop fretting." His hand swept over my bump. "How's the little one doing in there?"

"Restless today. It feels really low down, uncomfortable."

"I'm sorry, darling. Not long to go now. When do you see the midwife next?"

"January fourth. Really, it can't come soon enough now."

"Patience, Elizabeth. Let it cook properly in that little oven. When the sleepless nights start, you'll wish it was back inside you." He smirked.

"It. I hate having to call Bean *it*. I think Bean's a boy."

Sebastian's smile widened, his eyes lit up. "You think so? Oh, Elizabeth, I can still barely believe that I'm to be a father at last."

Pursing my lips, I nodded towards Bella who had plugged herself into her iPod.

"Of course," he said, "I'm already a father to Bella now, but you know what I mean."

I did know. He had longed for a child, an heir, with Libby but that wasn't to be. Falling pregnant with Sebastian's child was the greatest gift that I could give my husband. Even if I wasn't the first to carry his child, I was the only woman to make him a father. That had to be special, surely had to cancel out Scarlett's pregnancy.

Dizzy. My hand gripped a chair back as I sucked in a lungful of air. That poor unborn child. What had happened? How had she lost it? Unanswered questions but it wasn't the time to ask them. Not tonight. After Christmas. Part of me didn't ever want to know, wanted the whole sorry mess buried with the witch's remains.

Sebastian clapped his hands together. "So...the chapel. I suggest we all wrap up warm at eleven and pass an hour singing carols and saying our prayers. After, we can come back for hot toddies. Sound good?"

"Count me out, I'm afraid," I said. "I'll have an early night, if you don't mind. Also, it's treacherous underfoot and I really don't want to risk a fall."

"Quite so." Sebastian brushed a kiss over my lips. "Very sensible."

"Count me out too, I'd rather shove pins in my own eyes." Ruth quipped.

"Well, someone should perhaps stay home with Elizabeth–either you or Bella. Excellent. That's agreed. I'll walk over there now and see if I can fire up the oil heater so it's not too chilly in there."

This was perfect. I needed a little time alone in order to wrap Sebastian's Christmas present.

Alone in Sebastian's study, I smoothed out a small square of festive wrapping paper on his desk. I'd had to push aside his papers, he really was dreadfully untidy. I took from the pocket of my maternity smock, a small black box and lifted the lid. Bringing a hand over my heart, I placed the box onto the paper and smiled as my eyes misted with tears. I only hoped that my gift to him moved him in the way it did me when first I saw it. I'd had it made, you see. Cast from tin from a Cornish mine, the tiny metal horse was a minute replica of his faithful Zariya. The artist had totally captured the spirit of the mare, with mane and stance indicative of a horse mid-gallop.

Wiping my eyes with my sleeve, I cursed the volatility of my emotions these days and set about carefully wrapping the small box. Adding the final touch of a red ribbon, I tied a bow and sat back in my husband's chair. Job done. Tomorrow, I'd save it until last and hope that he loved it. Sitting forward again, I scooped up the waste paper and tossed it into the bin at my feet. Opening the drawer to my right, I replaced the scissors and turned my attention to shuffling his papers into some sort of order. There were piles of estate documents, tenancy agreements, invoices for repairs, and…wait a minute. The names caught my eye and, as I laid out the letter in front of me, I could scarcely believe what I was reading.

Dear Sebastian,

Further to our telephone conversation today, I confirm that I have put forward your preliminary offer for the acquisition of Evershaw Dove recruitment agency. As discussed, your proposal to acquire the remaining ninety percent shareholding, added to your existing ten percent, would indeed afford you full control of the business and ownership of all assets.

I accept that you are keen to purchase through a holding company and have, in this regard, today sent by separate cover, the relevant documents for your attention. Again, I have to advise you that you are proposing to pay far in excess of the current market value but note that you have declined to afford me the power to enter into negotiations with the directors on your behalf.

I will be in touch once I have received a decision in principal from either Mrs. De Montfort or Ms. Evershaw.

Yours sincerely,
Thomas Loveridge,
Loveridge Banks Solicitors LLP
Kensington, London W1.

Anger. No, not anger–disbelief. What the hell did this mean? My hands trembled as my body shook with rage. How could Sebastian do this to me? It was all falling into place: the mystery buyer that Ruth had spoken about. Of course he'd had this lawyer…this Thomas Loveridge, to do his dirty work and of course he'd gone to Ruth, not to me. But why? *Why?* I chewed my lip and tried to make sense of my discovery. Sebastian had bought ten percent of our company shortly after we'd met. Even that had been underhand - one minute I'd had lunch with him, the next he was in the boardroom negotiating his investment. At the time we'd welcomed his funding; we'd expanded, done very well. So, now…now he didn't trust us to manage his investment? Was it because I was absent, pregnant, a sleeping partner?

I'm pregnant with your child, damn you. Damn you to hell, Sebastian. Controlling, possessive, infuriating and manipulative man! This business was all I had. Mine. Well, mine and Ruth's. I did it without you. I will not be beholden to you for every aspect of my life, for every penny that I need. Not now not ever. We won't sell and that's final. This is something that you can't control.

With my mouth set in a stern line, I folded the letter and slipped it into my pocket together with the wrapped gift that didn't seem to matter now. Tarnished. Spoiled. Heaving to my feet I walked toward the door, intent on having this out with both Sebastian and Ruth. I stopped. I began to pace around his study. If I had this out with him now, it would undoubtedly lead to the mother of all fights and it was Christmas Eve. But, how could I keep this to myself when I was utterly fuming? No. Words needed to be said and I was ready to have my say as soon as he returned from the chapel. If he stormed out, so be it.

CHAPTER THIRTEEN

Closing the door behind us, Sebastian frowned. "What's wrong? The baby...."

"Is fine." I could barely control my temper, biting back the tirade had my fingernails almost embedded in my palms.

"Well something's up. Whatever it is, spit it out. Our guests no doubt heard you yelling at me the minute I walked in."

"Our guests, as you call them, are family. They have the right to know what a scheming...underhand *shit* I'm married to."

Sebastian's eyes darkened until they matched the twilight sky through the window of his study. "Shit? Did you really just call me a shit?"

"I did. And scheming and underhand, don't forget those words too."

Turning his back to me, my husband rolled his shoulders before placing his palms firmly on the mantle above the fireplace. "You have precisely one minute to explain to me what crime I am accused of now. Is this about Scarlett? The letter?"

"Fine. It'll only take me thirty seconds and no. As if finding out that you got Scarlett pregnant wasn't enough to cope with, I now discover yet another betrayal." Uncurling my fist, I thrust it into my pocket and withdrew the letter, waving in the air. "This. Explain this to me."

Sebastian glanced over his shoulder and looked at the piece of paper. "What is it?"

"Another letter, Sebastian. This time a letter from your solicitor to you, confirming your attempt to buy my company from under me. Explain that please." *Stay calm, Beth. Deep breaths, think of Bean.*

"I see. You've been snooping through my briefcase." His back straightened. His hands fell to his sides, he didn't look at me.

"Snooping, no. I was wrapping your present, if you must know, and I saw this on top of a pile of papers when I was trying to tidy up your desk for you. Talk."

He pushed a hand through his hair and turned to me, working his jaw, brow furrowed. "It was in my briefcase, but anyway, evidently you've read the letter, Elizabeth, so you'll know that I am keen to acquire the company, this is true."

"Acquire?" I laughed. "Take. You want to take the business from me so that I'm completely controlled by you…no money of my own, no reason to ever leave this… this *prison*." I spat my words, some meant, others not.

A flash of something–hurt perhaps–crossed over his eyes as they locked on mine. "You're wrong. You think this is about control?"

Not naturally submissive it had taken all of Sebastian's stoicism and patience to shape me into a wife who would defer to him in all matters. All matters except my business. That had always been non-negotiable, he'd known that from the outset, from the very minute he'd met me at a business event right here at Penmorrow. Had I ever given him reason to think that I would allow him to control that facet of my life? No. He was a minority shareholder, damn it. *How dare he do this.*

"Damn right I do. Everything you do, Sebastian, is about controlling people. Well not this time, no sir. This time you can't control me or my company. No sale Mister." Taking the edges of the paper, I tore it clean in half and then again, finally scattering the shredded letter about my feet. "You *know* how hard I've worked to build Evershaw Dove. What I sacrificed...my marriage to Alan, no time for my children...all of it. Years, Sebastian. Years of hard bloody work. Of blood, sweat and tears. And you think you can just waltz in and take it from me?"

"For twenty percent over the market value. That's hardly theft is it?"

Are you for real? "You just don't get it do you? I have nothing more to say to you." At the door I stopped and looked up at him. "Happy Christmas, Sebastian. Thank you for breaking my heart. Again."

His teeth bit into his lower lip, he shook his head. "Wait. You need to hear me out before you storm off, Elizabeth. There's more to it than..."

"No. There's nothing that you can say to make this right. We'll get through Christmas for the sake of the family, but after...I don't know. I'm afraid I don't trust you any more."

"I see." He looked crestfallen. "Very well, if that's how you feel."

I needed to breathe. Tears tumbled over my cheeks, hot stinging tears that wouldn't stop and I didn't care. You see, melded with my anger was a deep-rooted sense of guilt, always simmering somewhere deep inside of me. All the times I'd waved away my children when they were young; I was too busy or too focused on work to notice that they were growing up, until…until it was too late. The few precious years I'd shared with my son could never be regained. I'd been a terrible mother to him and then he'd been taken from me.

It all poured out and I welcomed the slow burn as I buried my face in a pillow in the sanctuary of our room. Only when I'd cried out all the tears and snot and misery and self-loathing, could I lie there. Looking at the ceiling. Wondering if life would ever be happy again. Thinking and overthinking until all I could do was to shut down my mind before I totally fell over a precipice. That's when I heard her voice.

A whisper - melodic, sweetest lilt that was somewhere distant, a cool breath on my cheek as though almost whispering in my ear. The words of a song. What was it? Ah, yes…rainbows, way up high, that's where I'd find her. I closed my eyes as the sobs gently ebbed away, replaced finally with a sense of peace, foreign, welcomed. In my mind's eye I saw a face that I recognised; I had seen her in countless photographs and in dreams. Libby De Montfort. Serenely beautiful, she smiled and stroked my hair. So sleepy now as she took my hand and led me up and away from the bed toward a brilliant warming sun. Soft grass tickled the soles of my feet, my toes. I was happy, so happy, her smile was infectious. We began to run, she set the pace, her hair golden, tumbling down her back, rippling with each step.

"He loves you, he loves you." She giggled and I giggled too.

The voice morphed into a deeper baritone, yet still a woman's voice.

Scarlett. *"Over the rainbow you'll find me too, my dear. I'm waiting for you, poor pitiful Beth. Nothing he ever does is good enough for you, is it? You couldn't even bear to hear his reasons, his motives, his generosity of spirit. Selfish. Selfish. Selfish…but the time is coming and retribution will be mine. Mine. Mine…."*

My eyes snapped open, beads of sweat on my lip and brow. My hands clutched my stomach.

Just a nightmare.

My child inside me was unmoving.

CHAPTER FOURTEEN

Sebastian

What the fuck did she mean by that? That we were over was reprehensible. Unacceptable. As I paced my study, the walls closed in on me as if the very fabric of my ancestral home was mocking, a voyeur of my demise. From the walls, painted images of my father, grandfather, older faces, all wore a smirk, knew better, would have done things differently, had the upper hand. Their scorn bled into my veins until my heart constricted and the air grew too thin to perfuse it.

When the toes of my boots struck mahogany I gripped the lip of a bookshelf and lowered my chin to my chest.

I. Would. Not. Accept. This.

Nostrils flared, chest heaved against the confines of my sweater, nails dug into wood and I swallowed down the tide of anger that frothed acrid in my throat. Anger at myself, at her for doubting me, my parents for the fucked up way in which they brought me up, at Scarlett...but predominantly at myself.

With one mighty sweep of a hand, I sent a row of journals somersaulting with a clatter to the wide oak floorboards, one striking my shin. Snarling a curse, I kicked at the pile of old books and furrowed my brow. This was ludicrous. I had every right to try and acquire her company. If she'd given me the chance to finish, I'd have told her what my motives were. Did she really think that I was at all interested in going into the recruitment business? It was laughable. Me. Did she not know me at all? I was all about control, she'd said, and she was right. I made no apology whatsoever for trying to control a situation that was set to destroy all that she'd strived for. My contacts in the city were fully versed on the the North American conglomerate who were set to strike at the very heart of her industry. Jesus, they'd already bought up most of Britain's largest firms, it was only a matter of time before they swallowed up all of Evershaw Dove's clients. It wasn't even about a hostile takeover or Black Knights. No. They were literally saturating the market; Ruth and Elizabeth would be drowned. Done for. Why did I fucking bother trying to pay over the damn odds for their business? So that I would face the financial loss that was sure to come, that's why–not them. They never would have known; they'd have taken the money and never needed to work again.

Raising my hooded gaze to the mirror above the mantel, I looked at my own reflection and saw my father's anger blaze in my own irises. Was I really like him? Wasn't love sufficient reason to act as I had? I would do the very same thing again. She was mine, Elizabeth. The stark reality was that there was nothing that I would not do to protect her. That would never change. *Never.*

I knew then what I must do. I would rise up, strong as age-old granite; I would be the rock of my family, damn it. My child, Bella, Elizabeth...all were mine and so they would remain forever. Nothing would break us. Threading fingers through my unruly hair, the anger fizzled and dissolved into the walnut of my eyes, replaced by determination and resolve. I was Sebastian De Montfort and I had the world at my feet. A child soon to be borne. A step-daughter, and a wife who possessed my soul.

A smile shaped my mouth. Time to be the man I was destined to be by my birthright. I would talk to Ruth and Elizabeth's mother. Get them on side. I came from generations of army men, strategists, officers. A war was only won by focusing on each battle, one at a time. One at a time.

CHAPTER FIFTEEN

"Calm down and talk to me." Ruth clutched my hand, seated beside me on a pew.

I looked at Mum, busy stirring a pot of something on the hob. She threw me a tight smile and asked Bella to give us a minute. My daughter sloped off, muttering to herself.

"Oh, Ruth. I'm worried. So worried."

"I know, love but think of the baby. Don't get yourself all upset like this, it's not good for the little one."

"It's not moving, Ruth. I *know* something's wrong with it. I had the most awful dream, and when I woke, I couldn't feel the baby move."

Ruth frowned and cupped her hands around my stomach. "May I? Let me gently push a bit and see if I can wake the little mite up." Gently at first, then more firmly, Ruth pushed and rocked my girth. "There. Did you feel that?"

Oh, thank God. "Yes. Yes I felt it."

"Little love's been asleep that's all," she grinned. "I may not have had kids, Beth, but I do know babies sleep now and then."

"Very funny. I was just worried. Sebastian. Where is he?"

Ruth and my mother shared a look. "He's upset Beth. He's talked to all of us and explained what's happened."

My eyes widened. "He told you?"

"About the business buy-out? Yes."

"I see. Well…you don't seem too shocked about it." I edged away from her and entwined my fingers protectively over my stomach.

Ruth's mouth curved into a smile. "Oh trust me, I was. Until he explained the circumstances, then I understood and, to be honest, it's an offer we need to talk about. Not now but after the holidays."

Recoiling, I looked aghast. "Are you kidding me?" Then to my mother, "Mum, am I the only one who sees what he's trying to do to me?"

Wiping her hands on a towel, my mother frowned. "No, dear but I do think you two should talk. He's a good man and, as your mum, I'd never stand by and let anyone hurt you, you know that. I think his intentions were good, when all's said and done."

"Great. What intentions were those? He's a prize manipulator who will say anything to cover his own sorry arse."

Ruth shook her head and tucked an errant curl behind her ear. "No he isn't. I agree, he's all guns-a-blazin' and his approach to some things is unorthodox, but he has a good heart, Bethie, and he loves you more than anyone in the world."

"In this world maybe." I couldn't shake off my dream of Libby, Scarlett. Why now? It was a nightmare that seemingly would never end.

"Listen, lady, and listen hard." Ruth lay a hand over mine. "You need to snap out of this funk. Yes, you both need to talk and I mean really talk, but right now it's Christmas Eve and that girl–your daughter–deserves a happy day tomorrow as do you. We all do. So, I want you to freshen up, come down and eat and then you and Bella can cosy up while His Lordship, your mum and I go stand in some draughty old chapel sniffing up all the skin cells of his old dead ancestors while singing Jingle Bells. Sound like you've got the better deal?"

Damn it, I'm smiling when I want to be mad at him. "Yes it does. I love you bestie."

"I love you too, fatty."

"I'm not fat, I'm pregnant." We grabbed each other in a clumsy hug.

Dinner was awkward. Sebastian sat directly across from me, studying me between every mouthful of venison stew. I didn't look at him, of course, I looked every which way other than at the rugged face of my husband, but I could sense his eyes trained on me. Chatter was light, of Christmases past at Penmorrow, of Bella's plans for next semester, of Mum's enrolment in a bridge club. Light unimportant chit-chat when there were hugely important things I really wanted to discuss but the elephant in the room loomed large and unmentioned. True to my pledge, though, I bit my tongue.

"Right. Who's for charades? We've an hour and a half to kill until church." We all rolled our eyes at Ruth. Such a kid.

"Okay. Let's go and play."

"I'll clear up here," said Sebastian.

I couldn't fight the disappointment, the irrational need in me to be close to the man who'd betrayed me and betrayed he had, no matter how he'd dressed it up for Ruth and Mum.

"I can do the dishes while you're at chapel," said Bella. "Come and join in, Sebi."

"Did I hear that correctly?" asked Sebastian. "Bella Dove is actually offering to wash up? Are you sick?" He chuckled.

Seems I'm the only one with a problem here. Fine.

In the morning room, I sat in the only armchair, leaving two expansive couches for the others. As badly as I ached to be close to Sebastian—for things to be okay—conversely I couldn't bear for him to touch me right now. The reaction of Ruth and Mum had been surprising to say the least. I began to wonder if it was all in my mind, that I was overreacting, being unreasonable, a stroppy pregnant cow. I was so confused. I mean, he didn't even try to deny his attempt to buy the business, not that he could; the evidence was thrust under his nose. But to leave it on his desk for me to see, pretend that it was in his briefcase? He'd wanted me to find it. He told Mum and Ruth about it, albeit after I'd confronted him. Nothing made any sense to me. Just how much more could he throw at me? How much more would I need to forgive him for before enough was enough?

My thoughts were interrupted by my family. Ruth and Bella got cosy together on the couch to my right, Sebastian and Mum on the opposite couch, to my left.

"Oh no you don't," said Ruth. "You're up first My Lord. Two teams: blue couch against yellow."

"What about me?" I asked.

"You're yellow. Bella and I are blue team and will still walk this even with just two of us." They high-fived each other.

Now this I have to see. Not one for games or silliness, Sebastian grumbled but rose to his feet and stood in the centre of the room, in front of the Christmas tree. He looked so awkward that I couldn't help but laugh.

"It's a book," he said gruffly.

"You can't talk!" I wagged a finger at him.

With a smirk and arch of his brow, my husband drew himself up to his full six feet, four inches and opened his palms to indicate a book.

"A film?" I asked, trying hard to not laugh again. Was it possible for love and hate to be so intertwined? Each raw and painful.

He gifted me with a smouldering stare, damn him. Two fingers were held up. In unison we all said, 'two words.' He nodded and held up one finger. First word. Pinching his index finger and thumb together, we all cried, 'the.'

"How the fuck did you know that?"

"No talking."

Oh, now this was where it got interesting. Folding over his giant frame, Sebastian bent low and swept his hand from his chin.

"A beard? Old man?" I was going to get this, make no mistake.

He shook his head and straightened up, stroking his jaw as he considered how best to act out the title of the book. Eventually, he stretched out his arms and dropped his chin to his chest.

Mother was the first to guess. "Is it The Great Gatsby,

Sebastian?"

Well, that was enough to send us all into fits of giggles.

"Mother, that's three words."

His arms still stretched wide, Sebastian looked at me. Our eyes locked, my fingernail tapped a tooth.

"The Bible," I said. A wild guess but the way his eyes widened, I knew that I'd guessed correctly.

"Yes. How the hell do you do that?" he asked, stalking back to the yellow couch.

"Well I knew it would have to be something monumental. It's not as if you'd ever choose something normal like a TV programme, 'I'm a Celebrity,' or 'The X Factor.'

"I may not be normal," he said, "but I'm yours, Elizabeth. Remember that."

Yes. Yes you are mine. I looked away.

As Mum's eyes grew heavy and she began to doze, Bella and Ruth took their turns. Sebastian and I competed to guess the correct answer and I beat him hands down. Strangely, it didn't feel good. All that I wanted was to be in his lap, enfolded in his arms, breathing him in. It was my turn to take the floor. As I tried to push up from the deep armchair, Sebastian sprung to his feet and helped me up. "Thank you but I can manage," I said in a harsher tone than I'd intended.

His mouth twisted into a scowl just as a loud clatter came from the hallway. "That was the front door knocker," he said.

"Whoever could it be at this time?" My eyes followed him as he strode from the room.

"Blessed carol singers," said mum stifling a yawn.

Voices in the hall. Male voices, Sebastian and...no. It

couldn't be.

"Damon?"

"My apologies Mrs. Dove. I…I've been walking for m…miles and no luck. N…no cars."

"The poor chap's half frozen." Sebastian reached for a woollen throw that had been folded over the back of my chair. Shaking it out, he draped it around Damon's shoulders. "Ruth. Please go and run a hot bath. Elizabeth, fetch a brandy. Quickly now."

He was ashen, his hair clumped and wet, his entire body shivering. Sebastian briskly rubbed the man's arms while Ruth and I hurried to do his bidding.

Returning with a glass of brandy, I carefully helped Damon to bring it to his lips.

Shit. This is all my fault. Whatever was I thinking letting him leave?

"I'm so sorry, Damon." I placed the glass down, its contents drained in one deep swallow. "We never should have let you leave this evening. You're frozen to death."

"Bath's ready," called Ruth from upstairs.

"Right. Let's get you in the tub, warm you up." Sebastian guided him from the morning room and took his arm as they ascended the stairs.

"Looks like we have a house guest after all," said Mum.

"Sweet." Bella looked a little too pleased about it.

"Hmm."

CHAPTER SIXTEEN

We gathered around the fire, all watching the flames curl this way and that; a pop and snap and soft roar were the only sounds in the room. The scent of pine, of forests and cosiness was pungent even over the aroma of warm punch that we sipped.

Our guest—the stranger who came in from the cold—had regained a blush to his swarthy cheeks but his disposition remained aloof. Bella stood beside him and, every so often, threw him side-eyes and smiled. I watched the pair of them with great unease.

"I imagine that none of you wish to go to the chapel now?" Sebastian looked at each of us in turn.

My mother spoke first. "I'd like to, if it's not too much trouble? It's not Christmas if we don't go to Midnight Mass and thrash out a few carols."

"Count me out," said Bella. Her face tipped up to Damon's. "Tell me you're not going with the oldies?"

"Bella!" I glared at her.

"Mind if I stay here and keep Bella company?" Damon purposefully asked Sebastian and not me. I was certain that he knew what my answer would be.

"No, that's absolutely fine," my husband replied. His gaze met mine. The fine lines at the corners of his eyes creased into a smile. "Are you staying here darling?"

I could lose myself in his eyes. In fact, I'd lost myself to him when first our eyes met, here at Penmorrow all that time ago. A lifetime ago, it seemed, when in reality it really was little more than a a couple of years. "Yes, I'll stay with Bella." *And keep watch on Damon.*

"Ruth?"

"Okay, count me in. I'll say a prayer for Beth and Bella. God knows they need it." She chuckled and kissed my cheek before going to fetch her coat.

"Sweet," said Bella rubbing her hands together and beaming at Damon. "I get first dibs on a movie."

I smiled and put an arm around my daughter's shoulders. "That'll be The Elf again then, love."

"Yeah, what else? It's Christmas Eve."

I wanted nothing more than to crawl into bed. The clock in the hall struck eleven long times before falling back into its steady beat.

Sebastian placed a hand on my arm. "A word please, Elizabeth."

I opened my mouth to fire back a smart comment, thinking better of it when I saw his dour face. "Okay."

He led me through to the library, perhaps to be somewhere neutral, or because it was where we had first met, I couldn't be sure. Shutting the door, he closed the space between us until he seemed to fill not only the air around me, but the entire room with his stature and his dark and brooding mood. "You're exhausted."

I shrugged.

Expelling a deep sigh, he gripped my hands and brought them to his mouth. He brushed a kiss over my knuckles before cupping my hands in his against his chest.

Please, no. "You hurt me, Sebastian."

I searched his eyes for signs of remorse. What I saw there, behind the amber flecks speckled against coal blackness, was sorrow. Love too, but his sadness broke my heart anew. Drawing my right hand from his, I cupped the sharp edge of his jaw and rubbed my thumb over his course stubble. "I love you, Sebastian, with all my heart. But…."

"But?"

"But, I don't trust you."

The heavy lids of his eyes closed tight and extinguished the amber light that had given me hope.

"Then there is nothing more to say." He let my hand drop and stepped back from me, the distance a chasm as our two souls were dragged apart.

"Explain," I whispered. "Tell me why you went behind my back…tricked Ruth and I. Why would you try and take from me the only thing that I've ever achieved in my life?"

"Your children. They aren't your greatest achievement? They don't matter?"

"What?" I recoiled from his words. "How dare you say that to me. How *dare* you."

He shoved a hand through his hair, dragging his fingers into the roots, tugging, eyes wild. "Your achievement is your family. Us. Our marriage, no?"

"Get out."

His large hands curled into fists at his sides. "I love you, damn it. I've only ever wanted what is best for you and the children.   Since…since she died, you've been my entire world. Every second of every day."

"Say it," I hissed. "Say her name. Scarlett."

His face was carved from ice.   One sharp slap and I would shatter him. "Yes."

"Say. Her. Name."

"Scarlett!" he hissed.

The door behind us rattled.   Branches of a tree scratched and tapped on the mullion window.

"She's the only woman you truly loved." *I can see it now. He may control me, love me in his own way, but his heart was always hers. Always would be. Libby and I had never stood a chance.*

"Lies!   I've never loved any woman as I love you, Elizabeth. Even Libby and fuck knows I loved her, really I did. It's you. You're having my child…everything I do is for you–for our family."

"And therein lies the truth." I stepped back and turned toward the door, reaching for the handle. "I'm a vessel for your heir. Nothing more, nothing less. It's a replacement for the child you lost."

"Don't.   Don't say that, Elizabeth.   Why won't you listen to me, let me explain?"

My stomach tightened into a knot of anguish as I shook my head. "Too late, it's done." Looking over my shoulder, I said, "go to the chapel and pray that you and I get through this."

CHAPTER SEVENTEEN

Sebastian

Scarlett. Would she always come between us, even in death?

The library was a desolate place to be right then. No less so because it had been the room where I had found her broken, Scarlett. Crumpled on that very rug before the fire with a book clutched in her hand, pressed to her breast. I'd taken it from her and seen that it was the family bible.

"Do you believe in God?" she'd asked as tears had streaked her face.

"I do," I'd replied.

"Then why would your *God* take our child from my womb?"

I'd had no answer to that.

CHAPTER EIGHTEEN

Without my husband's oversized personality and frame, Penmorrow took on an untenanted and somewhat desolate aura. Of course the house was dressed to within an inch of its façade, barely a surface remained free of garland or ornament, both old class and modern tat. Still the heels of my shoes clattered with a hollowness that resonated throughout the great hall as I entered to dress the table.

Above the chirping of The Elf drifting from the morning room, was a howling of wind that stole through crack and crevice; a symphony of noise that collectively was giving me a headache. Massaging my temples, I sat a while at the head of the table and surveyed the expanse of wood that soon would be draped in white linen. So much still to do. Exhausted. Downbeat. I needed to snap out of this dark mood for everyone's sake, not least of all for myself and Bean.

You might think me callous, a bitch perhaps, for not hearing Sebastian's motive behind his action. I know it too, and yet I can't explain how the discovery of his underhandedness was a body blow; how he crushed my confidence in his fist and threw the dust of my little empire in my face. I knew, sat there alone with my thoughts, that what I needed to do was to really listen to him. To trust in his love for me, and his protection and inherent desire to do me no harm. I knew this, I did, and still I cried and felt more insecure than I'd felt since the accident that killed Joe and Alan. In fact, the more I tried to analyse my own mind, I began to link these desperate feelings with how I had felt in the aftermath of that loss. Insecurity. Loss of control. Vulnerability. What woman didn't feel all of those emotions during her last trimester? Could it really be that my normal, hormone-fuelled emotions were exacerbated and inflated by grief? Add to that the fact that my marriage to Sebastian was in its infancy too.

You're not going mad, Beth, you're still grieving. Deep down you do trust him. You do love him, and you know that he loves you. You need to pull yourself together and not give in to this fear of being alone, of failure. Trust in him. Put your faith in him.

With a stoic resolve, I placed my palms on the arms of the chair and pushed myself to my feet. *Let's get this table ready for Christmas. Everything else will sort itself out. Whatever has happened in his past is just that: the past. The business is just a job, Beth. A job. Focus on what's important.*

A long shadow crawled over the pale Moroccan rug and danced over the pattern. My eyes widening, I brought a hand to my throat and turned to see what or whom had thrown its shadow into my solitude.

"Damon."

One side of his face was bathed in light, the other–the half of him that had already intruded into the great hall–

was twisted in darkness so that he appeared to be both angel and devil.

"You startled me," I said.

"I'm sorry. I just came to see if you needed any help?"

Before I could reply, the young man was at my side, in my space, his nostrils flaring on a sharp inhale almost as though he was breathing in my scent.

"No. I'm okay, thank you. I was just about to set the table for tomorrow." I turned from him, though not entirely, preferring to keep a watchful eye trained on this stranger in my home. "Aren't you watching the film with Bella?"

"She's gone to find some snacks." Taking a step to the side, Damon closed his hand around a neatly folded tablecloth and shook it out to its full length. "Let me help you with this. You shouldn't be stretching and straining in your condition."

Acquiescing, I moved aside and watched as he pushed and billowed the cloth until it fell in a white cloud into a perfect position on the table. With some care, Damon smoothed out any remaining creases until it really was quite perfect. I had to admit that I began to feel guilty at the way I had treated him, especially in light of the fact that it was the season of goodwill to all men, and so forth. I had become a wizened and suspicious witch. Honestly, the more I thought about the day's events, the more I shook my head at my own actions and emotions.

"Thank you, Damon."

His lips twisted up into a smile. "You're welcome." He stepped closer and held out a hand to me. "I know I'm a lucky fucker to have stumbled across your home and family and I'll always remember this Christmas. Thank you."

I looked down casually at his hand and placed mine in his tight grasp. Although a little shocked at his swearing, I was heartened to hear his gratitude. When he smiled, his face seemed to soften from the angular, dusky hardness of his Romany look.

"It's the least we could do," I nodded, slipping my hand from his. "And if you don't mind, I'd welcome some help setting the table. Why don't I call Bella to come and help and, between the three of us, we'll be done in no time."

"Sounds like a plan," he said.

"Wow. It looks amazing." Clapping my hands together I beamed at Bella and Damon.

"We're a good team," he said.

"It looks sweet." Bella adjusted the last sprig of holly that trailed down the centre of the vast table. "You staying for Christmas dinner tomorrow, Damon?"

Bella and I waited for his response. That had not been the plan at all and we certainly had not set a place for him, albeit almost half of the table was without place settings.

Tipping his head to the side, Damon fixed his eyes on Bella's. "Sadly not. I need to make tracks in the morning, if I can."

"But the roads…"

I chewed my lip.

"Hopefully they'll be clearer."

Drawing my gaze to the mullion window, I looked out into the night where a pillared lantern illuminated the driveway and plump flakes of white drifted in lazy swirls to coat the vista. I shuddered though it was warm in the great hall; the dying embers of an earlier fire at least took the chill from the room if not from my bones.

"We must see what the morning brings," I said.

"Yes. We must." His smile faded.

"Right," said Bella, "*now* can we please go and check the rest of the movie? I've made cheesy nachos and they're probably cold now."

My stomach growled. The baby gave a kick of approval.

Bella and Damon took the blue sofa in the morning room while I drew my puffy legs up and tried to get comfortable across from them. I didn't like or approve of the way that my daughter rested back against Damon's chest. They were way too comfortable for my liking. I tutted.

Damon looked over at me and quirked a brow. "Something wrong, Beth?"

His over-familiarity towards both Bella and myself stirred new anxiety inside of me. Bella pressed a button on the remote control and The Elf leapt into action on the television screen. Both turned their attention to the antics while I continued to watch them.

"Just that Bella has a boyfriend, that's all."

Both pretended to ignore me.

"Tell me about your parents," I asked.

Damon's head snapped around, his eyes darkening as they locked on mine. Bella sighed and paused the film again.

"My parents?"

"Yes." I tried to smile and lighten my approach. "What are their names? Do they work?"

His lips pursed in a taught line, and then: "Susan and

David. No, they don't work; they took early retirement."

"Ah, I see. What line of business were they in?" I reached for a nacho and dipped it in thick, gloopy cheese. Cold but delicious.

"Beth…with respect, Bella's keen to get the movie restarted. Do you mind if we chat in the morning?"

My brow furrowed in a frown. I took another nacho and shoved the dish towards them. "Sorry. I was just interested. And what do you do for work, Damon?"

"I'm a writer."

My brow arched. I hadn't envisaged that he was the creative type - more manual labour, his muscles were well defined beneath his tight-fitted top. "What do you write?"

"Mum. Can we please watch this?"

"Yes Bella, sorry."

Damon took a handful of nachos and fed one to Bella. My eyes narrowed.

"I mainly write horror," he said.

Why was I not surprised to hear that? "How interesting. Are you published?"

"I hope to be, one day."

"Do you have any of your books with you? I'd like to see."

"No. No, they're all at home."

"And where is home?"

"London."

"*Mum.* Jeez, it's like a bloody interrogation." Bella thrust the remote control towards the screen. The film restarted.

"Sorry," I murmured again. Nothing about Damon rang true. There was something…I couldn't put my finger on it. When I looked back at him, he was watching me with a gnarled scowl that quickly morphed into a soft smile. I looked at the television, my mind firmly on him. His words. His demeanour.

After thirty minutes or so my eyelids grew heavy. I was fighting sleep and losing the battle. The French mantel clock ticked half-past-midnight. Sebastian, Mum and Ruth should hopefully be back from the chapel at any moment. Deciding to await my husband's return in our bed, I said goodnight to Bella and Damon, in the knowledge that I wasn't leaving them alone for more than a few minutes before the others arrived back.

"Sweet dreams, Beth."

"Thank you Damon and merry Christmas."

"And to you too," he said as Bella leapt up to hug me.

"Happy Christmas, Mum," she said.

I kissed her cheek and tucked a lock of her wild hair behind her ear. "Merry Christmas, sweetie. I love you. Don't be too late to bed, now."

Alone in the hall, I looked back at the fireplace. From small hooks hung three stockings: Bella, Joe and Bean. All would be filled by the time my family awoke; small gifts lay hidden in a bag in Sebastian's study for just that purpose. And even though Joe wouldn't be here, eyes lit up in excitement, opening his stocking from Santa, I couldn't bring myself not to include him. As last year, I would drop off his presents to Barnardos children's charity in January.

The front door rattled on a sudden gust. I waited at the foot of the stairs, expecting the door to open and my family to appear. Nothing. Just the sound of the television. Gripping the banister for support, I heaved my laden and tired body up the first few stairs.

An icy breeze blew over my cheeks, whipping up the

ends of my hair. I stopped and looked up. All was as it should be. I climbed up further. How many times had Sebastian told Bella not to leave her window open? This old house was hard enough to heat as it was. A creak somewhere above and a cough behind me. I spun around and looked down to the hallway. There on the bottom step was Damon.

"What...?"

His eyes were trained on a point ahead of me, to the landing at the top of the stairs. His mouth curved in a smirk as his arm raised slowly from his side. "There you are."

Twisting on the stair, I turned to look up to the last two stairs at which he pointed. Nothing there. Back to him..., "who?"

His jet black eyes fixed on mine. "Scarlett."

CHAPTER NINETEEN

My fingers curled around the banister. Heart clattered against my ribs. "Scarlett? What the hell are you talking about? What do you know about her?"

Time stood still…yet the grandfather clock struck this way and that…a deep muffled ticking. Tock. Tock. Silence.

Bone cold, clammy, I tipped my head toward the top of the stairs. A blood red curtain blew on a draught from a shut window. Back to Damon. Closer, with a glint in his eye, the man climbed the first two stairs.

"I know all about her."

I shook my head. *Impossible!* "You can't. She's dead… Scarlett is dead."

His eyes creased in a smile–not at me but beyond. My head snapped back to see the target of his smile. A shadow passed across the landing as a shiver teased down my spine.

What's happening to me? This isn't real…

The man's finger stroked over his lip as his mouth curved into a smirk. "How does it feel, Beth?"

"What?"

"To live a lie?"

The air was cloying, my palm slick on the wooden rail. "What do you mean? What...what do you want?"

"How does it feel to steal another's life and lead it without a single thought for the pain and suffering you have caused?"

Blinking away tears. Needed to see clearly. "I don't know what you mean. You knew her?"

"Yes. I knew her. Better than you did."

"You're fucking insane...get out. *Get out!*"

"Mum?" Bella's voice.

Oh, thank God. "Bella. Call the police. Call Sebastian."

Her eyes wide, confused, "what's going on, Mum? Damon?"

"Do it!" Where to run? Upstairs trapped, downstairs him...

Frigid air. So cold. To Damon, voice aquiver: "Listen, whatever it is bothering you, we can talk it through. Sebastian...he'll be back soon." Voice dropping an octave, "Soon. And when he hears how you've frightened me, you'll have him to deal with."

His lips spread on a wide smile, eyes aflame. "Scarlett. Dearest sister. Do you hear what the whore says? She thinks the great White Knight will ride to her rescue." Throwing his head back, he barked a laugh, his features settling into a menacing scowl. When next he spoke, his voice was shrill like a woman's. "You fool. He's always been mine. You think by carrying his bastard child, that he *loves* you?" Maniacal laughter. "You took my life but not my heart. It beats on in *his* chest."

"No. No, please. Stop." *Think, Beth. Think.* "My

husband can get help for you…a doctor."

"I don't need a doctor, Beth." His words now a deep baritone. "She's here, you see. I'm a vessel for her, but she forbade me to be the one to end you."

As his eyes rose from mine, I turned. A wind whipped fierce as steel, cold as ice. Pressure on each of my shoulders, shoving. My footing…*NO!*

Thud!
Falling.
Tumbling.
Smack!
Bean…dear God…no.

Calm down, Bella…sweetie, don't scream; I can't bear the noise…my head hurts. Am I dead? I can move my fingers and toes and…I can see. The ceiling. Faces: Bella, Damon.

"Bella, run. Run for help." My voice, a croak.

"Argh!" *Pain: building and building. Can't take it. Feel sick.* "Please, help me. The baby…"

His face came closer, my eyes focused on his twisted smile. "Is it coming, Beth? Are you going to give birth to the new Messiah on Christmas morn?" He laughed. Closer still, he spat, "Karma is a bitch, isn't it. There's no way in hell that his spawn will live now, while my sister's rotting in the cemetery ."

The waves of pain subsided. Rolling onto my side, I rose up onto an elbow, eyes darting towards Bella as she tipped the contents of her bag onto the floor. "I can't find it. Where the fuck is my phone? Mum, oh God Mum, are you okay?"

"Sweetie, I'm okay but I think the baby's coming." Trying to calm my voice. "Bella. Try the house phone first. If it's not working, get the walkie talkie. If you can't find your phone, go and find the handset." Another wave built to a tight crescendo. My nails dug into my palms as I tried to sit, cupping my stomach. *"Shit!"* I puffed and I panted and I tried as hard as I could to breathe. *Sebastian! Oh, fuck. I need you...*

Behind me a key turned. The sound of a metal latch. A crisp burst of air that had me gasping as the pain subsided in a blessed reprieve.

The sound of his voice. "Elizabeth! Jesus Christ, what's happened?"

Damon's face withdrew. I tried so hard to sit, to turn, to see Sebastian's face. My mother cried out, Ruth cursed and there was mayhem and the pain came again and again, this time I screamed as pressure pushed down low in my pelvis. *Oh, shit! I'm going to pee myself. You can't come yet Bean. Too early...*sobbing now, I could scarcely make out whose voice bellowed over whose. Shouting. Ruth and my mum were upon me, their faces etched with panic but all I could see was Sebastian's long fingers stretched wide about Damon's throat, pinning the man to a wall. Every inch of my husband's body was taught as a feral snarl emanated from his throat.

"What the fuck have you done to my wife?"

Bella was sobbing and I wanted so badly to hug her. "She fell down the stairs, Sebi."

"Did the fucker push her?" hissed Sebastian.

"No. She fell but he was being weird–I mean freaky weird, saying shit about Scarlett."

Sebastian looked over his shoulder to where I lay, his eyes wild. "Elizabeth, are you injured?"

"I...I don't think so, no. My shoulder hurts and..."

The pain was building again. I sucked in a breath and bore down, a fresh wave of nausea and bile bubbling in my throat. "I'm going to be sick." I was retching and gasping and panicking. *Scared, so scared.* "What if it's not okay? Mum. I want my mum."

"I'm here dear. I'm here."

"Beth, listen to me." Ruth's voice. "Calm down. Pant. Do not push, you hear me? Bella, have you called an ambulance?"

Hysterical crying. "I was trying Sebi's number."

"Give me the phone."

Voices. Hands stroking my back as I curled forward, knees wide. "Fuck! Oh no! My waters…" *Please be okay, baby. I won't be able to bear it if anything's wrong. Please, Bean. Please.*

Sebastian's voice was pure acid. "Tell. Me. Why? Who the fuck are you?"

My own voice was little more than a whisper as my tummy relaxed. "Scarlett. He said she was his sister."

"Sister?"

Damon growled, struggling to reply under the weight of Sebastian's grip. "Your whore murdered my sister."

"That can't be true, she had no sibling."

"Yes she did. Damon Dorling at your service My Lord."

"And you came here…"

"For retribution for my sister, yeah. She's here, by the way, and she sees every fucking second of your betrayal."

I looked up to see my husband draw back his fist and slam it into Damon's face with a sickening crack. It was surreal. Blow after blow as he snarled, "you're insane. You're fucking insane. Scarlett's dead, you hear me?

Dead.   If you've hurt my wife…my child…I'll kill you with my bare hands."

"Sebastian, no! You'll kill him."

"Sebastian, stop!" Ruth bellowed, and then to me: "Ambulance and police are on their way but the roads are shitty. They want me to stay on the line." And then to my mother: "Hold the phone. Tell them what's happening and let me know if they have instructions." Ruth gripped my hand just as another contraction ripped through my core.   "They're on their way, Bethie.   Hang in there. Breathe through it."

CHAPTER TWENTY

Sebastian

I'd fucking kill him. Whatever he'd done to Elizabeth, I'd do ten-fold to him. I can't explain what came over me. I saw red, as they say. I saw my family broken apart again, a baby lost again. My fist took on a life of its own. Again and again I slammed it into his face; hours, days, weeks, years of anguish pumped my bicep as it drew back and forth and back and forth and I didn't know whom I was any more. I was taken over by all that was possessive, all that mourned and hoped and resented.

Her voice was what stopped me. Her sweet, charitable, loving voice. Voice of reason, of forgiveness. Still panic gripped me in a vise about my chest, my gut. I couldn't lose them, not this time. The red mist wound its way from my vision until all I saw was the terrified eyes of the man in my grip. Scarlett's brother? The poison of her genes was inherent within this man too. Two lost, twisted souls for whom there was no hope. Pity. Loathing.

And the baby...*my* child was coming. Finally.

CHAPTER TWENTY-ONE

Mum spoke into the phone, her spare hand threatening to break my fingers. "Hello dear, this is Beth's mother speaking. You'll have to speak up, it's a bad line. She's in a lot of pain. In my day a midwife would come. Oh, she is?"

Ruth's brow furrowed. "We need to get her up to a bed or couch. She can't give birth here on the floor. Bella, come and help me."

"No," barked Sebastian. "Bella, go down to the cellar and look for rope. Are you listening to me? Good. Through the first door into the main chamber where I keep my wine. To the left you'll see a coil of hemp rope on a hook. Bring it to me."

Jumping over my legs, my daughter ran to Sebastian's study, to the cellar. The pain ebbing, I turned my head and looked over at Damon Dorling. *Scarlett's brother. The evil lived on, would it ever end?* As my husband released his grip, the man slid down the wall, crumpling to the floor in a bloody knot of limbs.

Sebastian shook out his fist and rolled his neck. "Ruth,

out of the way."

My eyes widened as my huge bear of a man crouched low, his arms reaching behind and beneath me.

"No. You can't carry me...Sebastian, no."

'No' was not a word that this stubborn, darling man recognised. With a deep guttural growl, he lifted me up into his arms. I must have weighed a ton and yet he held me as though I weighed nothing at all, tight against his chest as I laced my fingers behind his neck. "She'll never make it to hospital at this rate. What the fuck do we need to do?"

"Get her upstairs if you can, onto the bed," said Ruth.

"They say only move her if it's safe to do so," said my mother, nodding into the phone.

"But, what about him?" I looked over at Damon's still form.

"He's out cold. I'll come back and tie him up. He's not going anywhere."

With Ruth and my mother bringing up the rear, he ascended the stairs. "I can't fucking believe this. If anything's happened to my child..."

"Calm down, Sebastian," said Mum, "she's only three weeks early, hopefully everything will be fine, the baby's cushioned in her tummy. We'll need plenty of towels and hot water. I watched every episode of 'Call The Midwife,' it's not that difficult, it'll just pop out. I had Beth in eight hours, and..."

"Mum!" I gritted my teeth. "Please stop talking like I'm not here." I pitied the person on the other end of the phone line.

With each step upwards, fear blossomed inside of me but, as another contraction clamped my stomach in its vice, stronger than the last, I buried my face in Sebastian's shoulder and bit hard on the soft wool of his overcoat, grunting through the pain.

The bed was a welcome comfort for my sore body. Ruth and Sebastian fussed, stuffing pillows this way and that. When I was settled as best I could be, Sebastian left to see to Damon. Ruth sat on the edge of the bed and placed her palms on my bump. "Is it moving?"

I nodded as Bean shifted very slightly inside. The pressure in my bottom increased, a leaden pain between my thighs. "I think he's ready. *Shit*, I need to push. Oh shit, it can't come yet. No, no, not yet."

"No you don't, lady. You keep that little one inside you until the paramedics get here. I know jack shit about childbirth, don't do this to me." There were tears in her eyes as she forced a smile and kissed my cheek. "I love you bestie, it's all going to be okay."

"You promise me?"

"Pinkie promise."

This was my third child. How long had Bella and Joe's labours been? Bella was nearly twenty-four hours, Joe was only three and a half hours. I didn't have long, I knew this. I sensed it. *Fuck!*

"Okay, I'm timing them." Ruth pushed a sleeve up and studied her watch with a frown. "Let me know when the next one comes."

"*Now,*" I hissed through clenched teeth as already another contraction ripped through me and stole my breath. "*Argh! Fuck, fuck, fuck*…I'll bloody well kill him if he thinks I'm ever going through this again."

"Shit." Ruth shook her head. "Right, we need to get you out of your knickers and get some towels under you."

"They're soaked," I wailed.

"I found some bath sheets," said Mum as she hurried back into the room, arm laden with folded towels, phone still pressed to her ear. "And I'll go and fetch a nice mince pie to keep your energy up."

"I don't want a sodding mince pie. I want this baby *out of me.*"

"Now now, Beth love. We all need to be very calm," said Mum. "That little girl will come when she's ready. How about a cup of sweet tea?"

"Oh my God, Mum." I honestly didn't have the will to respond to her. I was shaking. Badly. I didn't remember it hurting this bad, or feeling so rough with either of my previous deliveries. Shock perhaps? Fear, certainly. All my plans: the route to hospital driven at least a dozen times at my husband's insistence, and here I was about to give birth in Penmorrow, not knowing how my baby would be. I ached all over, I was tired, scared out of my mind and all I wanted was Sebastian's arms around me. "I want Sebastian."

"I should go and see how he's getting on. I didn't like the look of that young man from the get-go," huffed my mother at the door. "His eyes are too close together and he's got a smug look about him. Your father always said that no good comes of letting strangers into your house."

Ruth pursed her lips and gave my mother a look as Bella bounded into the room, breathless.

"Mum. He's gone."

"Gone?" Ruth shoved a hand through her tumble of curls. "What do you mean, gone? Sebastian's gone?"

"No. Damon. By the time I found the rope and got back, Sebi was out the front door, legging it up the drive."

With a gasp Ruth rushed to the window, wiping circles of condensation with her elbow. "It's too dark, I can't see him. Oh, wait. He's coming back but no Damon."

"What do you mean, 'no Damon?' Where's he gone?" My eyes grew wide and fearful, my hands stroked protectively over my stomach as another pain simmered before burning fierce deep inside of me, tendrils reaching around to the base of my spine. My fingers clutched the sheets, chin dropping to my chest as I grunted and puffed the pain away. It was all coming back to me, as natural as riding a bike. Blow. Blow. Don't push. Except I needed to push. Reaching out to grip my daughter's hand, crushing her fingers, I screamed, *"get Sebastian! I need him here right fucking now!"*

Coated in a sheen of sweat, I slapped at Ruth's hands as she fussed with towels and my knickers and all I wanted was to tear this baby out of my body before it split me in two.

"He's here. Sebastian's here, Bethy. Breathe the pain out…that's it."

"Elizabeth, darling. I'm here."

With a moment of reprieve from the pain, I lifted my face to his and bit back tears. I wanted to be brave, to not worry him any more than he was but I couldn't do it. "Is the ambulance here?"

Sitting on the edge of the bed, Sebastian rested his large palm on the shelf of my tummy and shook his head with a dour scowl. "Your mother's still on the line to them, telling them it's an emergency."

"Where is he?" I whispered, suddenly exhausted.

Sebastian worked his jaw, his jet lashes veiling his coal-dark eyes. "Don't you worry about him. I want you to focus on holding the baby in until help arrives."

"Hold it in?" I barked a laugh, incredulous. "It's coming, Sebastian and not even you can control that."

"Nonsense," he replied, furrowing his brow. "It's a case of mind over matter."

"Let me hit him for you," said Ruth with a tut.

"Where has he gone?" The thought struck me, amidst this utter madness and mayhem, that he could still be in the house. "What if he's here? Have you searched the house?"

"No, Elizabeth, he must have ducked up the drive. I hightailed after him but the fucker was too fast even in the snow. It's as dark as sin out there, I'll leave it to the police to find him."

Before I could reply, the tightening started...*no more, please*...I clawed at his trouser leg until his hand enveloped mine like a vice.

"Squeeze my hand darling."

This one was bad. *Oh my God, I can't...,* the pressure in my bottom was mounting. Throwing myself back against the pillows I drew up my knees as a roar melded with a scream that seemed to have no start and no end.

Muffled words. Crowning. A voice, mine, snarling like a banshee. *"Get it out of me! Please...Ruth just get it out."*

As the waves subsided leaving an undercurrent of pressure and ripples of pain, I gasped and sobbed and then realised that it was Bella who was crying and not me. My mother's voice was trying to cheer her up. It was exciting, she said. Soon meet your new sister. Ruth snapped at her—ask for an update on the ambulance, she said.

When finally I focused on my husband's face I saw

pure, unadulterated fear and anger. He turned to Mum and Ruth. Ruth was down the messy end while Mum was cuddling Bella. "You women must know what the hell to do," he snapped. "This cannot be normal…to be in this amount of pain. *Do* something."

"I can't feel it moving."

Quickly climbing onto the vast bed beside me, Ruth parted my thighs further and squinted and frowned. I didn't give a thought to how humiliating this was. I wanted this baby born now. "Beth, love, I think you need to push. Do you think she needs to push?"

My mother spoke into the phone and nodded her agreement. "Yes love. See if you can push her out now; poor poppet's probably getting tired too."

"What does this mean?" Sebastian's voice was clipped, anxious. "It's not good is it?"

"It means your baby's coming is what it means. Where's that ambulance?" Ruth seemed to have towels everywhere–a sea of towels and hands stroking my stomach and eyes on me and…

"Here it comes! I'm pushinnnggg! Ah, God damn buggering fuck…"

"Language Elizabeth!"

He didn't go there. He seriously did not fucking go there.

"I can see a head!" Ruth grabbed my hand and forced it between my legs to my apex where a soft, warm, wet mound was stretching and burning until my eyes pricked with tears.

"Dear God…*hair! I see lots of hair!*" His head twisting this way and that, Sebastian was riveted.

"Pant now dear. Let the head crown."

"Mum...I can't...I can't bear it."

"Yes you can and you will."

I panted and puffed and gripped Sebastian's hand as he beamed, tears clouding those gorgeous jet orbs of his.

"They're five minutes away," said Mum, phone to her ear. "Yes well hurry up, my daughter's about to give birth."

Oh shit, here it comes. I bore down with all my might and determination. Down into my bum with a slow pained groan that rose octave after octave as I felt my child's shoulders pop and slither and then...*it's out!*

Silence.

A baby's cry–small and angelic.

"Here it is!" Ruth's hands were full of blue and pink flesh and dark bloody curls. "Congratulations!" she cried as the baby was hastily wrapped in a towel and placed on my chest.

CHAPTER TWENTY-TWO

Sebastian

At that moment, all the gods opened their skies and all that I could see was the glorious gifts of their offerings. Riches beyond this world: wisdom, honour, all that was good. As if the deities perceived my pain and reached down from high and draped my weary corpse in robes of gold and delivered to me a panacea to ease my suffering. The child was there. Real. Hair and eyes and fingers and toes and nothing mattered more than he.

A son.

CHAPTER TWENTY-THREE

Through a haze of tears and sobs of relief I laughed and looked up at my man who looked utterly shell-shocked.

"It's…"

"A boy, Sebastian. You have a son." Everything else in the entire world dissolved at that moment. All I could see was elation etched over Sebastian's chiselled face, and our son. Our *son* in my arms.

"I have a son." First he looked at me and then he asked Ruth, and then my mother and Bella. "I have a *son?*"

"Yes my darling," I wept. "*We* have a son."

He was the most beautiful thing I had ever seen: eyes the colour of honey, contrasted by dark chocolate curls framing an elfin face that radiated all that was good in the world…in *our* world. As hot, happy tears ran in rivulets over my cheeks, I studied each minutiae of this newborn angel. The way his nose quirked up ever-so slightly at its tip, the soft cleft in his chin and the faintest hint of a dimple to his left cheek which mirrored Sebastian's. He was the essence of Joe and nothing like him and my heart swelled with love and broke all over again from a tight band constricted by longing.

Down at the business end of me, Ruth wiped away her own tears with her sleeve. My daughter and mother were hugging each other while Mum repeatedly expressed her shock that her predicted girl was in fact a boy. Then, suddenly: "They say the ambulance and a midwife are here, Sebastian."

A hammering on a door sounded somewhere way beneath us. "Bloody typical," growled Sebastian. "About time. Bella, go and let them in and see if the police are with them."

In moments, the room seemed to be full of people, of faces.

"I'm sorry it took us so long to get here. The roads were pretty diabolical. Police are waiting downstairs." A gangly male paramedic nodded to Sebastian.

A midwife called Sue, in blue scrubs, was quick to take over. "You've delivered a baby," she told Ruth with a smile. "You should be very proud of yourself."

"It was nothing," she quipped back. "Like shelling peas, hey Beth?" Ruth winked and grinned at me but I knew that this had to have been the scariest thing ever to have happened to her.

"Right, let's get the cord clamped and cut."

"Can my husband cut it?"

"Certainly he can."

Deftly a male paramedic opened a sterile pack beside Sue as she snapped on a pair of blue latex gloves. A clamp was retrieved and quickly applied to the cord, while Sebastian's face was a picture. I really thought he may pass out at any time.

"I can't...I can't hurt her," he said with a frown, his

mouth sculpted into a tight line.

"Darling, you won't hurt me. I won't feel a thing, I promise you," I reassured him.

With great care and a discernible shake to his hands, my husband snipped through the umbilical cord and blanched a pallid grey. "Fuck," he groaned. "That was disgusting."

Ruth and I gave a short laugh but, the truth was, I couldn't have been prouder of and for my husband. I cuddled our newborn to me. "Look at our son: the future Lord De Montfort."

As my mother snaked her arms around Sebastian's waist, she too cooed and melted at our new addition.

"Looks like a fine baby," said the paramedic. "How are his lungs?"

"Loud," Sebastian replied. "He squawks like a fox caught in a trap."

"My son does not squawk." I smiled, contented, relieved.

Cramps low down inside me stole my breath. Resting back onto the soft stack of pillows, I steeled myself to deliver the afterbirth, trying to remember the sensation of its passing. To my left, the room seemed to be filled with noise and chatter and uniforms.

"Here it comes," said Ruth, her voice shrill. "You take over, Sue, I've no bloody clue what I'm doing."

Sue moved swiftly, years of experience shaping her face into a confident smile.

"What the devil's happening?" At my side now, Sebastian gripped my hand, his gaze levelled on the action that was unfolding down below. "No…it's not…"

"Not what?" I squeezed his hand tightly as my body

expelled the slimy lump that was the placenta.

"Twins!" His head snapped round, eyes wide.

Oh my God! Snorting a laugh I shook my head. "It's the afterbirth, silly."

"Jesus!" he exclaimed as he tipped his head back and laughed too. "It would seem that I have rather a lot to learn about this childbirth and parenting business." Shoving back those broad shoulders of his, he let go of my hand and threaded his fingers through his tousled raven hair. "I'll go and talk to the police while you...," he waved a hand towards my lower half, "get sorted out."

"Good idea," I nodded. "And Sebastian? I want him found." My eyes narrowed, lips set firm and determined. "I can't rest until I know that nutcase is locked up."

With a curt nod he left the room.

"Is he okay?" I asked the midwife as she checked over the delivered placenta, depositing it into a yellow bag. "I had a fall...is he hurt at all?" I held my breath and watched as Sue lay my son on the bed on a fresh towel and peeled back the soiled one to scrutinise every inch of the baby.

"He's absolutely fine from the looks of him," she replied, producing a stethoscope which she pressed to my son's tiny chest. At that moment, the baby's lip trembled - proceeding to a loud cry that had his little fists curled tight, knees drawn up so that he was again in a foetal position. "Nothing wrong with his lungs," she chuckled. "Heartbeat's normal and temperature's fine. He's got all the fingers and toes he should have and there's no sign of any distress or injury. All in all, I'd say he's perfect."

And breathe...

"Mind if I check you over, Mrs. Dove?" The more

gangly of the two paramedics ran skilled hands over my body, finding no injuries other than a blossoming bruise to my sacrum and a small egg on my crown.

"Does this little fella have a name yet?" asked Sue.

"Yes, what did you both decide for a boy?" Ruth chipped in.

"Please don't tell me you're giving him some convoluted awful De Montfort name like Giles or Siegfried," said Mum wiping tears from her cheeks.

What? "Heavens, no."

"What about Alfie?" asked Bella as she peered over Danny's shoulder and chewed her lip. She was quiet. Too quiet.

"I'm not calling your brother after a You Tuber," I huffed. "No, we haven't decided on names. Why don't you give him a cuddle, love? Meet your new brother properly, then you can see what name you think would suit him."

"You're alright." Her eyes locked on mine for a fleeting moment, long enough to see the conflict in those pools of blue. She looked away. "I'll go and see what's going down with Sebi and the cops."

"Bella."

"Yeah?"

"No-one will ever replace Joe."

My daughter tensed as she reached the door. "I know."

"But we'll love this baby for who *he* is. Same as we loved Joe, we'll love this little one too, okay?"

"I know."

"And Bella…."

"Yeah?"

"Merry Christmas darling."

"You too."

To say that I was sore was an understatement of epic proportion. I'd slept for, I don't know, a couple of hours or so, until the little one wailed and I latched him on to my breast and sat there in bed, enthralled as my child suckled from me as if milk was soon to be rationed. His appetite evidently matched his father's.

Ruth and Sebastian were being evasive, sharing no information on Damon's apprehension other than to say that the police were dealing with it. They were treating me as though I were made of glass and might shatter with the slightest touch of trouble but the truth was that I needed to know that we were safe. Their silence led me to assume that we in fact were anything but safe, that Scarlett's brother was still at large, a threat to me and to my children. I was edgy therefore when, at a little after eleven o'clock, I made my way downstairs to the kitchen. The late morning sun had draped the entire house in gold and there was a stillness in the air, an expectancy almost, but of what I didn't know. In my arms I cradled my son, tightly swaddled, sleeping. In my mind I harboured a dozen questions.

"Elizabeth, why aren't you in bed?"

Dropping a kiss on the baby's soft head I smiled at my husband from the doorway. "I'm not sick, Sebastian. It's Christmas Day, I want to be with my family."

Sebastian worked his jaw as he walked over to us and lay a palm on his son's tiny pink hands. His eyes creased in a loving smile. "Your mummy is as stubborn as a mule, my dear boy. You'd better get used to the fact that she's the boss around here."

I laughed. "I don't think there's anything further from the truth, do you?"

Those dark eyes glittered as Sebastian smirked. "Hmm, well I have let you get away with a great deal, Lady De Montfort. However, now that you're no longer pregnant you'd better prepare yourself for retribution."

Oh my...

"Is that so?" I bit my bottom lip and swallowed down the sinful thoughts that sprung to mind.

"It is so, yes. Don't think that I haven't made a mental note of all your misdemeanours and brattish behaviour."

"Brattish?" I threw him a coy smile. "Oh heavens, I have no idea what you're talking about."

Leaning in, he kissed my cheek so that his stubble grazed my skin and tugged my core. His scent of sandalwood and musk was a heady combination. I licked my lips as a blush crept over my cheeks.

Before Sebastian could respond, voices drifted in from the hallway as Ruth appeared, Mother in tow and behind them a uniformed police officer.

"Lord Sebastian?" The officer extended his hand to my husband who gripped it in a firm handshake.

"Yes, good morning and merry Christmas to you."

"And to you too, Sir." He gave a nod to me. "Lady Beth I presume?"

Gosh, I'll never get used to being called by my title. "Yes, hello."

Smiling at the baby, the plump man with scarcely a peppering of hair over gleaming head took out a card and handed it to Sebastian. "My apologies for intruding on your Christmas but I thought you'd like an update on this Damon Dorling fella."

"Let me take him." Mum took the baby from me as Sebastian led the officer, Ruth and I to the morning room where we sat, though it hurt me to sit, and listen to what he was about to tell us.

"I'm Duty Sergeant Bill Ferris." Tugging at the creases in his trousers, the man sat and looked at my husband as if I wasn't in the room. "I've got some preliminary results of our enquiries into Damon Dorling and I'm afraid it doesn't make very good reading."

"How so?" Sebastian reached for my hand and placed it on his thigh, fingers laced with mine.

"Well, until six months ago he was detained under The Mental Health Act in a long-stay psychiatric hospital in Leicester."

The fine hairs at my nape prickled. I squeezed Sebastian's thigh. "So he was mad like his sister?" I felt my husband's leg tense beneath my palm. "How the hell did he get out?"

Sergeant Bill nodded, his expression dour. "I'm not able to go into too much detail about his clinical diagnosis other than to say his was a complex and challenging case by all accounts."

"Schizophrenia?" asked Sebastian.

The officer tipped his head, eyebrow raised. "It's interesting that you ask that." He hesitated, and then: "I don't suppose it would hurt to say you're not far off the mark. He was on a day excursion–part of his therapy– when he gave carers the slip."

Sebastian's brow creased in a deep frown, his fingers slipped from mine as he rested his head in his hands. "Fucking wonderful."

Wrapping my arm around Sebastian's waist I shifted

closer to him and asked the officer, "and if you don't find him?"

The man chewed his lip, fingers drumming silently on his knee. "We're doing our very best to scour the area including the beach and the woodland on the estate. I've got an officer in the village too."

"And if you don't find him?" I repeated, patience wearing thin.

"Then we'll post an officer here if that's okay with you both?"

We nodded in unison.

"Find him," said Sebastian, voice clipped.

CHAPTER TWENTY-FOUR

They didn't find him. It was no surprise to any of us that Damon Dorling seemed to be long-gone who knew where. Christmas lunch was a subdued affair. In light of our arrival it should have been a time of celebration, instead the conversation was somewhat stilted and strained, champagne barely touched.

"Will they send someone to the house?" I pushed my plate away and looked down at the half-eaten turkey and swiped the paper crown from my head.

Sebastian eyed my plate with a frown. "You should finish that, Elizabeth. If you're to feed our son, you need to be well nourished. And yes, I believe an officer is to be sent up this evening."

With a roll of my eyes I speared a sprout and threw Sebastian a dry smile. "Always so bossy."

His lips sculpted into a grin as he winked and said, "on the contrary. I'm looking out for your interests as I always have and always shall."

"And I love you for it," I replied. Behind me, in a wicker basket on a chaise beside the fire, a soft whimper escalated to a cry. "I'll go."

"Oh please," said Mum, "let me. It's time for a proper grandma cuddle." Returning to the table, my mother swaddled our son tightly in his pale buttermilk blanket and lay him gently against her shoulder, her hand lovingly cupping his tiny bottom as his cheek pressed into her neck. "What's your name to be then little lad?"

I glanced across to Bella and caught a smile tracing her mouth.

You will love him, darling. Give it time.

Her eyes rose to meet mine and softened as I mouthed, *I love you.* 'I know,' she whispered back and she did know. She knew that she was loved beyond words by us all and that no baby could ever mar the bond that we shared, she and I. Life had been so very hard for my daughter, for all of us, and it had taken months for her to pass a single day without crying after the accident. Now though, with her burgeoning love for Theo, son of Sebastian's estranged friend, Marcus, it seemed as if she had turned a corner and could finally see a future bathed in light rather than darkness. Or perhaps that was a mother's wishful thinking. For now she seemed content and she'd adapt to life with our new addition. Mostly she was away at university anyway.

"Freddie."

Everyone looked at Sebastian.

"Freddie?" I repeated.

"His name. The baby. I like Freddie."

Silence.

"Like as in Frederick–Fred?" asked Ruth with a smirk.

"No. Frédéric after the first Lord De Montfort, Frédéric Louis. But we shall call him simply Freddie."

"I like it." *Freddie.* Studying the newborn's features, the name fitted him like a second skin. I beamed at my clever husband as the rest of our gathering all rolled the name on their tongues and nodded in unison. "Yes. Yes, let's call him Freddie."

"Freddie De Montfort," said Ruth with a wide smile. "Very noble sounding."

Sebastian looked deservedly smug. "Freddie it is then." He drew back his shoulders and puffed up his chest. "Master Freddie Horatio De Montfort."

"Wait! *Horatio?*" My eyes narrowed. "No son of mine is being called Horatio."

"Shut up! Hor-ratio?" quipped Bella as she tipped up the end of her nose with her finger. "Very posh."

Sebastian's dark brow furrowed in a frown at us all. "I'll have you know that the late, great Horatio, first Viscount Nelson, first Duke of Bronté shares that young man's lineage."

"Who?" Bella reached for another roast potato, dropping it like a doodle-bug into a sea of gravy on her plate.

"Bella Dove! Did you not study history at school?"

"Chill Sebi, geesh. I probably skived that lesson."

I cut her a glare as did my mother.

"You're related to Horatio Nelson?" Ruth's eyes widened.

"Tenuously, yes," he replied. "His moniker - 'England expects that every man will do his duty' is one that I've long since advocated. I've now done my duty." With a dazzling gleam in his sparkling jet eyes, he pointed to his son. "And there he is."

I couldn't help but chuckle. "I don't remember it being

a duty for you when we made him…"

"Elizabeth!"

All eyes were on me as a hot blush burned over my cheeks. "Just saying."

Master Frédéric Horatio De Montfort, one day Lord and heir of Penmorrow, was duly named.

The meal cleared away by Ruth, we gathered in the morning room, Bella distributing gifts from beneath the tree. Sebastian was wearing that very same smirk that he'd worn when first we'd met. On that day, many moons ago, on a cold autumnal day, he'd draped a loser's medal over my head. I may have been the very least adept woman in business at the team-building day, but little did I know then that I'd be sat here in the same house on this day, as that gorgeous man this time draped a fine Tiffany & Co. Diamond pendant around my neck, the heat from his fingertips permeating my breastbone. I thanked him with a kiss and decided that I couldn't love any man more than I loved Sebastian. Yes, he was pedantic and underhand in much that he did but his love was steadfast, undeniable, tangible.

"Open this," I said, thrusting a small box into my husband's palm. "I hope you like it."

After he had torn away the paper and the box lid and taken the small tin horse into his hand, I saw the heart of the man I loved. A tear spilled from his eye to be swiped away with words of thanks. But I saw it. Zariya lived on in the gift and I smiled at how it touched the tough man that was Sebastian.

As I held Freddie to my breast, his small face and my modesty shielded by a shawl, I looked over at my family with a sense of possessiveness and raw instincts of protection and preservation that sat heavily in my stomach like a clenched fist around a rock. Nothing. No-one. Would hurt my family again. Not while I had breath left in my body.

The water was heavenly. Somewhere downstairs–it could be a thousand miles away right now–Christmas afternoon was unfolding. Here, in my sanctuary, I lay amidst a heady scent of bergamot and geranium. Each tender spot in my battle-worn body relaxed and yielded its ache. Tendrils of my scruffy up-do clung to my neck and shoulders, eye lids pressed softly closed as thoughts of our baby, our children, floated and bobbed in my mind. I had become adept at blocking negative thoughts, anxieties, in the quest for calm. Ten minutes. Just ten minutes of relaxation with no thoughts of that man or his long dead sister or trauma or Scarlett or anything other than my son. My husband. My family. Was it too much to ask that the part of my brain that took all the bleakest thoughts and tucked them in a corner, that it would quieten and let me be? Yes. Tendrils reached out from the dark part of my mind and took me right back to the time before Freddie, before pregnancy and before marriage, to a place where my life was threatened and I was mad and disbelieved. To a time when my dreams were haunted by Scarlett, by the poison of her ministrations. Long dead perhaps, but her ghost lived on, of that there was no doubt in my mind. Here? Was it possible that the hand of some rotting corpse, her putrid spirit, had pushed me down the stairs, or had it been simply wrong-footing? I questioned everything. Her brother: equally as vile and evil, had tainted not only this festive day but his hand and perhaps the hand of his sister had hurried my son into this world and for that I would never forgive them. Never rest easy until both were gone. Where was he?

I sank lower into the bath until I was submerged to my chin, the water warm but my bones cold. My eyes opened and I stroked a hand over the empty cavern of my belly, swollen but soft. From the corner of my eye a movement…door handle turning so that candlelight reflected off the brass sphere and danced there a while until the door opened and the handle fell into shade. I sucked in a breath and held it.

"Are you okay darling?" Sebastian. *Thank God.*

Scooting back and up, I shaped my mouth into a smile to mask my fear and nodded. "Just trying to relax a bit."

"Mind if I join you?"

"Since when did you ever ask permission?"

Silently, reverently, Sebastian shrugged off his black dress trousers and unbuttoned his snow-white shirt that he'd donned for our meal. I watched his long fingers deftly pop each fastening and marvelled at the chiselled definition of his abs and the course matting of black hair webbed over his chest. In the soft light, my husband's beauty was illuminated, transcended to God-like as he towered so tall that the bathroom seemed to shrink in his presence. I too felt small. Childlike. I hugged my knees, eyes locked on his as his naked form folded into the bath, water sloshing this way and that and my heart rattling in my chest.

"Come," he said, arms open to receive me like a deity about to cleanse a sinner.

I moved swiftly and without question, eager to feel safe in my protector's arms. He drew me into his lap, cheek pressed to his chest so that his own heartbeat boomed steady in my ear. His arms wrapped around me like steel yet warm and familiar. I realised that the only place that I ever felt safe was right here, melded to Sebastian like a second skin. The crown of my head received a soft kiss that lingered, his breath tumbling over my face like a whisper of silk.

"You're trembling." His hold on me tightened, to banish the chill inside me.

"I'm scared."

His thumb and finger pinched my chin to tilt my face up to his. His brow creased in a frown. "If you're worried about that bastard, Damon, then don't be. The police will find him and he'll be locked back up in the asylum or wherever it was he absconded from."

"But what if…"

"What if nothing. Don't question me, Elizabeth. If I say that you're safe then you are safe. I would protect you and our children with my life, you know this."

*You couldn't protect me from Scarlett. You couldn't stop my son and husband from being killed…*I mustn't doubt him this way. *Stop it Beth.*

"Is the officer here?"

"Not yet."

"But it's dark outside."

"It may be dark but it's not late. You're not alone, so stop fretting."

"Freddie?"

"Asleep. I had to prise him from his sister's arms."

A wide smile crept over my face. "Bella was cuddling him?"

"Yes, darling. I think she's rather taken with her

brother."

"Oh, I'm so relieved." That was the best news ever. "We need a monitor so we can hear him," I said after a pause. "The house is too big, he's too far away."

"Darling, he's in his crib at the foot of our bed. The bedroom is barely thirty paces from here. Close your eyes and think of the angel that together we have made. Isn't he the most exquisite child you've ever seen?"

Blowing out a sigh, I smiled and settled in his arms. "He really is. Did you see that he has your dimple?"

Sebastian chuckled and stroked a hand over my stomach, letting it rest on my pubic bone. The nearness of his fingertips sent a current to my core. "I noticed that," he replied. "And the noble De Montfort nose too."

"Beak," I quipped with a short laugh.

"Beak, hmm?" His fingers traced a lazy circle over my stomach.

My breath caught at his touch. A tightening deep inside me was painful; a yearning to be as close to him as it was physically possible to be, while cramping so badly that I squirmed in his lap. Needing more, wanting less.

His mouth close to my ear as he grazed the crook of my neck with his bared teeth. "I love you my darling." Punctuating his expression of love with a chaste kiss, he rested back and loosened his hold on me. The void where his arms had held me securely left a cold chasm.

"And I love you Sebastian." I covered his hand with mine.

"We need to talk about it. The business," I said after a few moments.

Sebastian expelled a sigh. "It was never about control, you know."

"Please explain it to me. I need to understand."

His arms encircled me again, the rough of his chin grazing my shoulder as he told me everything. And when he had finished and as I tried to absorb the enormity of all he'd said, I realised. Sebastian would never betray me. In his fucked up way, all that he did was for me. For us. When would I learn to trust him? To accept that, for him, control was his coping mechanism; without control he felt weak, afraid even.

"I understand." I did. "Thank you, my love, for protecting me."

"But?"

"But, you have to let me stand on my own two feet, Sebastian. Whatever happens to our business has to happen at my hand–at Ruth's. I can't look back and have regrets, blame you, resent you. Do you see that?"

"I see my stubborn, wilful girl."

"Please, Sebastian. For me. I've come too far, risked too much, worked too hard to walk away now. I'll either be very wealthy in my own right, or very poor. Either way, I will have done it myself. No help and no blame."

"You're insufferable."

"I am, but I'm yours."

"Mine."

Our lips met in a tender kiss. He tasted of cranberries and vintage wine and love and all flavours familiar and wholesome.

I shivered when at last we parted, the water tepid, cloudy.

"And Scarlett? The child?"

Looking into his coal-dark eyes, I could see that his own insecurities matched my own. "I have to learn to accept it. It will take time."

Sebastian gave a dour nod. "Thank you. I'm sorry," he said quietly. "Now, let's get you out of here. If Freddie's anything like me, he'll already be thinking about his next meal."

I snapped a sharp salute and smiled. "Yes Sir."

My husband chuckled as he stepped from the bath, while my body yearned for him; I was needy and vulnerable, determined and stoic. Inside, I was a tangle of emotions and a knot of anxiety. Taking a towel, he wrapped me up and rubbed me dry; I was a child, he was my Daddy, my Master, my lover and my salvation—indulgent and strong. I lowered my gaze and submitted to his benevolence. He was all that was good and all that was bad, wrapped up in a towering slab of muscle and skin and the heady scent of power. Mine. His. Us.

Bone dry, he took my hand, a towel sitting loosely on the deep V that carved a downward path through wisps of black hair. It was hard to tear my gaze away. He led me from the guest bathroom along the corridor as soft peals of laughter drifted up the stairwell on tiny particles of dust that settled on a carved eagle atop the banister post. My eyes met those of the mahogany bird, his two scratched orbs unseeing yet watching me. I looked up at Sebastian's back, at the flex of his muscles, the breadth of his stride. Our bedroom door was open, all was quiet, not even the soft breathing of our son. Across the expansive room, past the four posts of the bed to the crib at its foot, nothing stirred.

"Should I wake him, do you think?" Shrugging off the towel, I slipped my robe from the arm of a wing-back and pulled it on, shivering in the chill air.

"Let him sleep," said my husband. "I'll lay here with him a while and bring him to you when he wakes. Go and join the others and I'll be down soon."

"If you're sure." Truth was, I really didn't want to be parted from him. My son was just a few hours old, every second spent with him was a chance to get to know him better. "Perhaps I'll just pop downstairs for a few minutes," I conceded. Tiptoeing lightly, the soles of my feet whispered over board and rug until I was close enough to peer at our baby and to see him sleep.

His blanket was over his head.

My breath caught. Mother's instinct screamed and alarm bells rang hollow in my head. I tore back the blanket.

The room spun.

The cradle was empty.

CHAPTER TWENTY-FIVE

Sebastian tore at the little sheets and tore at his hair. The hairs at my nape rose. My skin crawled.

I left him then, snatching at his clothes, ramming feet into jeans as curse after curse roared from his lips and all I wanted to do was to scream.

My fingers curled around the eagle's neck, splintered feathers, the cold wooden sentry holding fast to his post as I bent over the top stair and shrieked my family's names one-by-one until they scurried like ants beneath. "Where's Freddie? You have him?"

Each looked at the other in turn and then at me, heads shaking.

Behind them a knocker rapped once, twice, thrice.

Behind me a voice boomed. "He's gone."

"He can't have gone," said my mother.

"What do you mean, he's gone?" asked Ruth.

"He's not in his fucking crib." Sebastian shoved past me, long-legged leaps and strides. Stairs two, three, four at a time.

The knocker clattered on wood again. *Rap rap rap.*

"Bella, get the door.   Ruth, go with Elizabeth and search the upstairs bedrooms."

A newborn baby does not vanish.   This cannot be happening. Everything around me was a whirl of colour; spinning. My arms encircled my waist, hands clapping against my sides as tendrils of hair lashed at my eyes, my cheeks. Bitter wind stung my skin, sucked the breath from my lungs and on that wind all that I could hear was a baby's wailing and a voice, shrill, laced with devilry. *"Rock-a-bye baby, in the tree top.   When the wind blows, the cradle will rock. When the bough breaks, the cradle will fall…and down will come baby, cradle and all."*

The wind stopped blowing.   The voice was nothing more than a haunting.   Below me, a man stomped snow from his boots and tucked gloves in a pocket.   Beside me, Ruth rubbed flat palms down the length of my arms and said my name over and over again.   I was conscious of my heartbeat and marvelled that it could function while broken.

"Just in time," I heard someone say.   And, "we need to find him, he's just a few hours old."   A man's voice, the one with the stomping boots, spoke. "I'm the officer assigned here this evening.   When was the child last seen and where?"

Hands motioned towards where I stood, to the eagle, to the wall sconces and beyond to the bedrooms.   "Our room," I croaked.   "He was sleeping in our room."

"Come on love. Let's start searching the bedrooms like Sebastian asked."

I barked a laugh.   "You really think Freddie got himself out of his crib and is playing hide and seek?"

My friend's eyes misted.   Her lips pursed.   "No, love.

But we need to do something."

"Scarlett." Even her name tasted toxic, acetic.

"Scarlett's dead, Beth. Stop this...stop this now."

We held hands, Ruth and I, as though we were young girls exploring a haunted house in a game of dare. From room to room we moved swiftly, silently. Behind curtains and doors we looked. Under valences and chaises and dressers and trunks. We called his name and we listened and said nothing at all.

In the belly of the house beneath our feet, doors crashed, footfall thundered and my husband's rage seeped through the entire fabric of Penmorrow, into my very bones until I was at one with his fury and my teeth bared and I shook with the need to destroy and maim.

I couldn't see and I couldn't think. I didn't even think that I was breathing any more.

Ahead of me, where the corridor ended blunt and final, I saw a trace of white; a figure, or perhaps a mist or my imagination or a dream. It beckoned, I thought. And then: clarity.

The roof.

Dear God, no...

"Get Sebastian," I hissed. *"Now!"*

She ran, calling for Sebastian, for the police officer, while I walked towards the mist, the light.

The door that led to the stairs that led to the roof, was ajar. My palms pressed to cold stone as I climbed the steps, so narrow was the space that I couldn't outstretch my arms or even turn. I could only climb up. And up. And up. The door at the top was also ajar and it was thump-thumping against the frame under assault from the elements outside. Bracing myself, I pushed it back and stepped out onto the uppermost point of Penmorrow. Beneath my bare feet, tiles cut a lattice into my soles but I didn't care because there...there was my son.

CHAPTER TWENTY-SIX

Damon Dorling curved a smile and dropped a kiss on my son's forehead. As a single tear wound its way over my cheek, all I could see was Scarlett the night that she took her own life from that very spot. The look of absolute acceptance on her face was a mirror of Damon's resolve. The inky mess of hair that framed his face, eyes that glittered and the arrogant jut of his chin.

"Please. Give him to me." My words carried on the wind. I wasn't sure that he heard me. Beyond the pitch of the roof the sun was snuffing out, crimson and chalky mauve. Twilight sucked a bat from the rafters. It careened and swooped as Freddie cried for me. My hands rose from my sides as I stepped closer. I saw my child, the pain of his distance unbearable. Behind me wood splintered and a presence cast a shadow over the tiles. My eyes locked with Damon's. I watched transfixed as he took my child from his chest. His arms straightened so that Freddie was held aloft over the precipice like a sacrifice to a God who wasn't seeing. Who didn't hear my silent prayer. Who had forsaken me. *Give him to me...please God, give him to me.*

"Don't."

He was a gypsy. A waif devoid of a heart. He dangled my son over the cold stone turret toward the last glimpse of twilight. Towards the last mocking swirl of the day as it melded with tree tops and was gone. Darkness tugged at my fingertips as they grasped at the void between us. "Please. He has his whole life ahead of him."

The shadow stretched long and tall and wide. Sebastian. He stepped beside me, in front of me, and the rage burned off him effervescent and fierce. I was a spectator in my own child's destiny. Another shape. A man in uniform, abstract and foreign here on the rooftop above Cornwall, above the world as it continued its normal life. Arms encircled me, the scent of friendship, of Ruth, of my mother, my daughter. Gasps. Sobs. We were all there to witness the life or the death of a child. The start or the cessation of my own life. The air grew thin, all was silent.

Sebastian's movements were lithe and slow. Somewhere in the distance an owl flapped his great wings and launched himself into the night sky with a mighty *to-hoo* and still my son hung helpless above a sheer drop onto rock and moss and death.

"Ah, the great Lord himself."

I reached for Sebastian's hand, tried to lace my fingers with his. His own fingers curled into taught fists at his side.

"My fight is not with you," said the man and, in the moonlight, he tipped his face to me in a blue-white smile. "Come here Beth."

"Stay. Where. You. Are." Sebastian took a single step

to the left, his body a wall that marked a boundary dividing good from bad, between myself and Damon. "Give me my son."

From the darkest shadow the policeman walked, palms raised. "Everybody calm down," he said as though it might solve things. "Sir. Let's have a chat about what's troubling you shall we? Let Mrs. De Montfort hold the baby and you and me can go and find a nice glass of something strong downstairs."

Damon Dorling snorted a laugh that shook his shoulders and the baby so that Freddie's arms and legs extended, tiny fingers spread wide in alarm. A mewling cry drifted over the rooftop, above treeless hill and gnarled forest beyond. Snow fell in gentle quiet sheets like life itself was folding onto us layer by layer. "There's nothing to talk about," he said. "Nothing that will change this lad's fate. A life for a life…hey Beth."

"I'm here," I said, shaking off Sebastian's hand from my arm as I passed him by. "Take my life. You think I'd want to live without my son? Another son's life taken by your fucking bloodline?" I was calm. Don't ask me to explain it because it was not a rational feeling. Or perhaps it was nothing more than a fundamental and inherent need in a mother to protect her young; I would die for him. I was about to die for him. For Freddie.

"That's a fair swap. Come closer." Holding the child in one bird-bone hand, Damon beckoned me closer and I went to him.

"Elizabeth, *no!*" Sebastian's anguished cry, the sound of his heart tearing in two, the officer's barked command—none of it mattered. A crisp wind whipped open the edge of my robe exposing my breast. That too, didn't matter.

The sound of a radio crackling between broken bits of speech behind me as the officer spoke in hushed tones of code and orders and requests for urgent back-up.

Too late. Too little.

I was close to him, my son, one pace more and he would be in my arms, held to my breast, suckling. I was snatched around my waist and lifted from my feet so that my toes dangled and my arms flailed. *"Put me down…."*

Sebastian's arms closed tight as he hissed, "Never. I will never let you go. *Never."*

A pale buttermilk blanket slipped from Damon's arm leaving Freddie exposed. Suspended in one hand. Cold. Shivering. Nothing but a scrap of a child. My entire world. With a guttural snarl I twisted and bit Sebastian's palm, springing free to rush to Damon, to Freddie. My hand outstretched. The child slipped. Cold seeped into my bones. A silent scream shaped my mouth. I looked down. Freddie was in my arms.

"Give him to your bastard husband."

Oh, thank God. Thank God. I wept and kissed our son's head as Sebastian was upon me, arm snaked around my waist, the other cupping Freddie's head as father kissed son again.

"Take him." Kissing my son as if for the last time, I lay his cold body in my mother's arms. "Take him by the fire. Do it. Quickly." To Bella: "get blankets and a hot water bottle. Ruth, there's a baby thermometer in Freddie's nursery next door to our room. *Hurry!"*

The three dearest women in my life scurried off with looks of grave concern and tears and shock. I turned to face Damon whose head was tipped to one side, a finger playing in the air conducting some unseen and unheard orchestra. My mouth was dry. Heartbeat rattled like a freight train against my ribs. Jaw clenched tight, I narrowed my eyes and all that I wanted was to shove him from the roof. Sebastian was upon him before me. The police officer—evidently giving up all hope of a peaceful resolution—drew from his belt a small canister, waving it menacingly toward Damon, toward the night where nothing stirred and nothing saw but us.

My husband's mighty fist pistoned from his side to encircle Damon's throat. With his weight behind the grip, the slighter man arched back over a turret with a shriek and it was odd. I wanted him dead. I didn't want another life taken. My fingertips burned with a need to claw out his eyes. My mind told me that he was sick. Needed help. A hand grabbed Sebastian via a fistful of sweater, pulled. Snapped orders and barked warnings and a scuffle. *What to do. What to do.* My hands tore at my hair. I glided closer. Strange. I couldn't feel my feet, my legs. I was cocooned by a mist, a light. Libby. It couldn't be. Almost melodic whisperings in my ear that it would be okay, to trust, to believe.

Ahead of me the scene played out like a theatrical production. Fisticuffs. Cursing. Hopeless. Utterly hopeless. And then…he broke free and rubbed at his throat, gasping, laughing. His eyes locked on mine, Damon. It was just he and I, as if no-one else was there on the roof of Penmorrow except me and a vessel of pure undiluted evil.

"No, sister. Leave me be. Leave me be." He spoke into the wind, eyes darting this way and that. "I'm not. You do *not* have the monopoly on rooftop drama." He was talking to himself, every word spoken punctuated by a puff of mist from his lips. "Everything I do," he snapped, "is for you. Always for Sarah-Fucking-Dorling. Parents' pet. Should have kept me, not you."

In the furthest corner of my eye, Sebastian and the officer seemed to dance out an old Edwardian musical comedy while directly in front of me Damon Dorling punched the air. "Then it was always *him*. The lord. Never *me*. Never your flesh and blood. Well let's see how the lord is at flying…."

Damon's fist connected with Sebastian's jaw with a sickening crack. Somewhere above us wings flapped and the night came to life, alarmed. The officer was pulling at Sebastian, at Damon and beneath us the sky lit up with flashing blue and white that made paper cut-out silhouettes of the trees. Curses and sirens and my darling love was waist-high bent over the turret.

"Stop." A small voice came from myself and it grew and grew until I screamed, "*Stop!*" and he did. He let my husband go and in that time that he took to register my cry, handcuffs were snapped shut about his wrists. He was brought to his knees there on the rooftop of our home. Sebastian. My heart, my soul, grabbed me to his chest and I hoped right then that he would never let me go. His scent: sandalwood and musk, his breath on my face, his coal-dark eyes searching mine. It was over?

"Elizabeth," he said. "Elizabeth."

"Sebastian."

The night air was electrified with sirens and lights and uniforms but I saw only my darling husband's eyes that were unwavering from mine. Never before had I witnessed such pure love as I saw that night high above the Cornish coast in a world that was marred and broken and pure and good.

CHAPTER TWENTY-SEVEN

Damon Dorling was taken away that night. A lost and broken soul, he would likely spend his foreseeable future in a secure mental health hospital. Police shared with us that night, more about his troubled past. The parents who had given him away aged nine, keeping only their daughter Sarah. She'd been less trouble. Less volatile. How that must have played on his mind over the ensuing years. The treatment that he'd received and would receive again. Would it help him? Part of me wondered how much of his devilment was learned and how much was inherent in his bloodline. Was it possible that he and his sister Scarlett were both schizophrenic, as the police had said, or did Satan have a hand in the carving of their destiny? Whatever your beliefs, I knew what needed to be done for the sake of peace in our lives.

Father Peter stood in the centre of Scarlett's small room deep under the belly of Penmorrow that Boxing Day morning. It was a bright and mellow day in England, in Cornwall, in the lands surrounding the ancient walls of the house. Here, though, the air was oppressive, as dark as the priest's robe. Dipping a small oak aspergillum into a wooden chalice, he recited the Apostles Creed and blessed Penmorrow. Blessed us. You may give no mind to what I'm about to say, but as holy water splashed over the small iron bed, stripped of lace and her, over her mirror, her walls…the air was scented and fresh. It was as though I could breathe again.

Sebastian's hand grasped mine and, although I knew that he had only consented to this—what he called 'mumbo-jumbo'— for me, I'm sure he sensed it too. That rugged, chiseled, beautiful face of his finally settled into a peaceful smile. He nodded once and brought my hand to his lips, gifting a loving kiss to my knuckles.

"It's really over, isn't it?" I asked.

"It is."

"Now we can be a family again."

"I love you Elizabeth De Montfort."

"And I love you so much it hurts my heart, Sebastian."

Above us, Freddie's faint cry rang out as the grandfather clock struck ten. Bella's laughter and my mother's shout of 'don't spin him around, you'll shake his brain,' confirmed that all was finally as it should be. Nothing was perfect. We were fractured. Somehow, though, I knew that as a family we stood stronger than ever. We were survivors.

CHAPTER TWENTY-EIGHT

Sebastian ~ Three Years Later

Through the maze I chased him, Freddie, a tangle of raven curls bobbing as he ran. Finally, the errant toddler was within my grasp and I clutched him to my chest, dropped to my knees as I was.

"Do you have any idea, young man, how much you are loved? How long I have waited for you?"

"How long, Papa?"

"A very long time, my darling boy. An eternity."

"And now?"

"And now I will keep you for as long as I live." Glancing up at the grand façade of Penmorrow. "Until I'm as old as our home and until your mother and I are one day grandparents. And then…and then I'll watch you, son. I'll still love you even when I'm no longer here. When I'm but a distant memory and your mother and I are high up there on a cloud together."

He and I tipped up our heads in unison and gazed at the ribbons of cloud threading past the sun.

Gripping his slight shoulders I levelled my eyes to his. "I want you to remember something. Life is rarely fair. Life is hard but if you find love…then nothing can ever harm you. Love is magic, Freddie. It gives you the power to overcome anything; to turn darkness into light."

"Really?"

"Yes son. You see, love is extraordinary. Love knows no boundaries, no lies, no reason. Love is blind and yet love sees all. Love, Freddie. There is no greater gift than the love of one's family."

"I love you Papa."

And as deer skittered across the grass and a dozen swallows rested awhile atop the old oak tree, I was at last content.

Home.

Penmorrow.

The end.

CHAPTER TWENTY-NINE

If you've enjoyed this book, please shout about it on social media. Please also leave a review; reviews are the life-blood of authors. Thank you.

Thank you for following Beth and Sebastian's journey. Who knows if this is the last that we will hear of them. If you'd like to read more of their life, then let Janey know via social media.

Connect with Janey here:

Twitter: @JaneyRosen

Facebook: facebook.com/janeyrosen

Instagram: JaneyRosen

Email: janeyrosen@yahoo.com

Blog: janeyrosen.me

14551386R00089

Printed in Great Britain
by Amazon.co.uk, Ltd.,
Marston Gate.